THROWING MY LIFE AWAY

LIZ CZUKAS

Throwing My Life Away

LIZ CZUKAS

ALSO BY LIZ CZUKAS

Ask Again Later
Top Ten Clues You're Clueless

AS ELLIE CAHILL

When Joss Met Matt
Call Me, Maybe
Just a Girl

To my high school friends,

who would have done it for me.

[1]

TWO WALLS DOWN, two to go. The blankness in front of me is jarring. I can't remember the last time I saw this much of the paint color. I'd sort of forgotten what a nice blue my bedroom is. For years now, the color has been more of a picture frame around everything I had mounted on the walls.

If you're picturing boy band posters or kittens hanging on clotheslines, you're way off. I wouldn't sacrifice that kind of wall space to cute stuff—feline or British. Nope, I preferred to look at my room as a gallery. It was like a puzzle, fitting photographs between postcards and leaving just the right amount of space for my academic decathlon medals to hang without covering up the photo of the team. The collection of hand-drawn birthday cards from my artsy cousin mounted in a square with a frame of flower leis from the luau themed party I'd had for my sixteenth. Every photograph I had in my high school paper, carefully clipped and hung in a column beside the door. A blank piece of sheet music with lyrics written across it in my best friend's distinctive handwriting.

My personal museum. And now I'm dismantling it. Against my will.

A rap at my door startles me and my mom pokes her head in. "How's it going, Mariska — oh my gosh, look at that!" She steps the rest of the way into the room and gives the empty wall a smile. "Wow. What do you think?"

I think it sucks. I like my room the way it was—is? It was like living inside a collage of my life. "It's weird," I say instead, because my mother and I do not see eye-to-eye on my walls. My mother is the poster child for letting go of the past. She's like a permanent After on one of those home organization shows. The anti-hoarder. Totally devoid of sentiment. Anti-mental? That should be a word.

"It's kind of soothing, don't you think?" She approaches the wall with a squint. "Hmm. These walls are going to be fifty percent spackle by the time I finish filling all these holes."

I fight the urge to press my back to the wall and spread my arms out protectively. "You're not doing anything until I'm gone!"

She laughs. "I know, I know. We had a deal. You really can leave all this stuff here. I promise I'll be careful taking it down."

"No. I want to do it myself." Because I don't trust

her not to throw away the things she doesn't realize are important — which is all of it. Also, because I want to take as much of it as I can with me to Loyola University in two weeks.

Two weeks. My stomach rolls. How can the summer be nearly over?

"Well, keep up the good work." My mom waves over her shoulder as she goes back to her own purging in the living room. I would never be doing this if she wasn't already on one of her redecorating benders in the rest of the house. She can't stand to leave the walls the same color, the furniture in the same places for too long. She says it's like an itch in the middle of her brain, crying out to be scratched with new color and change.

The only change I've ever really liked is the kind you drop into a piggy bank.

Two weeks.

I would like nothing better than to put everything back on the walls in the places I found them. And maybe panic for a few glorious hours. But I know that's not really an option. So the only thing I can do is try to keep as many of my treasures safe as possible. My mother has taught me the method well enough. Sort everything into categories — keep, toss, donate. So far, I'm really only good at keep. I could win an Olympic medal for keeping things.

Down on the floor, I've got boxes, theoretically one for each category. But I'm in serious danger of overflowing the Keep box. And that's before I tackle the last two walls. Not to mention the rest of the room.

Maybe if I mention that Olympic medal idea to my mom, she'll be more receptive to me keeping most of my stuff. Or, you know, everything.

From behind me, my laptop chirps. I hurry to the desk chair as messages from Sun pop up. She sends me a rapid-fire series of messages. In order, they make a live-action comic strip of sorts. The first is a shot of the door to the restaurant where she works. The second is her giving the door the finger. In the third, she's holding her name tag with a lighter underneath it, as if to burn it. The last is a picture of her tan forehead and a giant towel turban. The attached message is: *Drumroll, please!*

Her last day as a waitress was yesterday, and she's celebrating the end of the employee dress-code by dyeing her black hair some wild color again.

Color? I type.

I get another picture in return. One of her old stand-bys. A shot of Sun holding one finger up in admonition. I take it to mean I'm going to have to wait and see.

I use my phone to take a picture of one of the blank

walls in my room and send that to her.

I get back a gif in return, some celebrity I can't immediately name doing an exaggerated WTF take on the set of one of the late night talk shows.

I type, *I know, right? It's hideous.*

Did you call the police? You've obvious been robbed.

Smiling for the first time in a while, I reply, *I suspect aliens.*

A terrible drawing of a UFO with a smiling alien in it is the only reply.

What's up tonight? I need to get out of here.

You pick. This is obviously a traumatic day for you.

This is why I love my best friend. She may not be the wall collage artist I am, but at least she knows how much I am hating this. We make plans for her to pick me up later and I leave her to her elaborate hairstyling regimen.

Footsteps on the stairs send me flying out of my chair again. If my mother pops her head back in, I cannot look like I need help. I absolutely do not want her in here for this. She will try to talk me into getting rid of way too much. Which is anything, in my humble opinion.

She does tap on the door again, this time holding paint samples. "I'm going to Home Depot to get a few test colors. What color do you want in here?"

"What's wrong with the color it is right now?"

She sighs, looking utterly dejected. "It's the same color you've had since you were twelve years old."

And that in itself is something of a miracle. Before the current, calming blue color, my mom repainted my room as part of her regular redecorating rotation. My room has been pink, yellow, gray, pale green, a weird color that was called adobe, but was an exact match for that disgusting circus peanut candy....

"I like it."

She frowns slightly. "How about if I just bring a few colors in the blue range?"

"How about you don't paint it at all? I know I'm going to college, but it's still my room."

"I'm going to have to paint it after I fill all these holes."

A little ball of frustration tightens in my chest. I don't want her to fill the holes. I certainly don't want her to paint it. I'm about to be unceremoniously dumped into a cinderblock dorm room with a roommate I've never met before, who will probably want to murder me in my sleep. There will be no color on the walls in my future murder scene. I want to die knowing my room at home is at least the color I left it.

These are obviously totally rational fears.

My mom is still looking at me expectantly.

"Fine. Try to get the same color."

She rolls her eyes. "I'll do my best."

When she's gone, I set to work on the next wall, dragging my small army of boxes along with me. My stepfather, Ray, gave me a stack of flattened bankers' boxes to sort my stuff into with a reminder to set aside anything with personal information on it to be taken to the commercial shredding plant where he takes all that kind of stuff. A few years ago, Ray had his identity stolen, so he's a total nut about it now. So far, my shredding box is empty, but I still have my desk to tackle.

I pull the pins out of an 8x10 picture of the staff of the paper, The Arrow River Chronicle. This is one of my favorite pictures of all time. We'd all crowded into our faculty advisor's convertible, much to his dismay, and he used my old camera to take a picture of all of us. You can't even make out everyone's faces with all of us crammed into the tiny car, but the ones you can see are all laughing. God, my abs hurt from laughing by the time we were done, and I'm not even sure what was so funny.

Which is really the best kind of laughter, if you think about it. I can almost feel it vibrating through me again now and, despite my mood, I'm smiling. Mr. O'Neill had refused to take more than one picture, even though everyone had done their best to dig camera phones out of their pockets. He'd declared my old 35mm SLR camera the most likely to take a decent picture. Plus, I'd left it carefully settled on the ground before attempting to climb into the car. My cameras were like my babies.

So this is the only shot.

Which reminds me—Sun demanded I print another copy for her before she leaves for Fordham in New York. I have to find the negative, and see if I can get back into Arrow River's darkroom before she has to move. My file box of negatives is in the top drawer of my desk, and I retrieve it now to look for the right strip.

But I hesitate with my finger on the latch. I know if I start looking at pictures I'll never finish my room. So I set the entire file box inside the banker box I'd scribbled *High School Memories* on. I have to keep my negatives with me at Loyola. I don't trust anyone else to keep them safe.

Although that will put them in reach of my probably-secretly-a-thief-in-addition-to-being-an-ax-murderer roommate…. See? Nothing but rational, normal fears.

The picture of the newspaper staff joins the negatives in the already partially full box, and I go back to pulling pins. Photographs, all my Academic Decathlon medals, quotes I've clipped from magazines or printed out in fancy fonts. Everything I'd surrounded myself with over the course of my life is being boxed up.

I hate this.

People keep saying that college is this great adventure. That it's going to be the best days of my life. But what if they're wrong? It could easily be awful. Nobody says it, but it's just not statistically possible for everyone who goes to college to be happy, is it? I could be one of those people who hates it. Who never fits in and can't even finish school. What if I flunk and I have to leave at semester? Would that be the worst thing? Not if I'm miserable and lonely and no one likes me. What if I don't have friends as awesome as my friends are right now? What if I don't have friends at all? What if there's no vegetarian food in the cafeteria and I starve to death? Or like, get scurvy or some other old-timey disease and no one even remembers how to treat it? That could happen.

My laptop chimes again and I quickly abandon my task to check what came in. It's email this time.

RE: Hey Roomie!

It's from my future roommate. Her name is Briony and she enjoys football and exclamation points. We've emailed a few times as we figure out who's bringing what to our room. She's bringing a microwave, a speaker dock, and a DVD player. I'm bringing a refrigerator, a TV, and a strong sense of impending doom.

Today's message says:

Two weeks! I'M SO EXCITED!! Can't wait to meet you!

My mom wants to know if you're allergic to nuts because she'll leave them out of the brownies if you are! Let me know ASAP, k?

See you soon!!

- B

The brownies? Is this some Loyola tradition I'm not aware of? She used the definite article, so I feel I'm supposed to know about these brownies. And how soon will she be making the brownies if I have to let her know ASAP. Do the brownies have to be two weeks old?

I hit reply.

No, I'm not allergic.

After a few minutes of contemplation, I add,

Thanks for checking. See you soon.

Three more minutes pass before I change the last period to an exclamation point. I can't find a spot to put in any all-caps declarations. In the middle of dismantling my room, I'm about as unexcited as I've ever felt about college. Apparently, I'm the only eighteen-year-old in North America who isn't.

I'm so nervous. I type. *What if we hate each other?* Then I delete all that and just hit send, realizing the instant it's gone that I didn't even sign it. Shoot.

Maybe I should go back to packing. It's pretty clear I'm not meant to communicate with other humans right now.

[2]

BY THE TIME Sun picks me up, I've nearly finished with my room. I can hardly believe it, except that my whole body is sore from all the lifting, moving, and reaching over my head.

After I fawn over her newly red hair for an appropriate amount of time, we decide to see a movie and it takes all my concentration not to doze off in the theater. You'd think giant robots and explosions would do the trick to keep a person awake, but you'd be wrong. Sun, on the other hand, thinks I am much better entertainment than the movie. She keeps waiting for me to fade out, then carefully sets as much popcorn as she can on my head and shoulders. Then she pokes me in the knee and laughs as they all rain into my lap. It would be completely annoying if she weren't laughing so hard. It's hard to get mad at someone who is giggling so much no sound is even coming out.

Normally, we'd go hang out at our favorite diner, or back at one of our houses after the movie, but it's obvious to both of us that I'm not going to last much longer. She drops me off at home and I practically drag myself to the bathroom to brush my teeth before falling into bed.

Even with all the lights off, my room feels different with bare walls. I didn't realize how much my posters, photos and all the other stuff I'd used to cover the walls had buffered the sound. The slightest rustling of my sheets echoes as I try to settle myself. The faint glow of streetlamps through my window is brighter, too, reflecting off the wide expanses of pale blue. It makes me feel cold, despite the summer heat outside. I burrow deeper into my blankets and focus on letting exhaustion make its way from my limbs to my brain.

Why is it that when you've got the time and the will to sleep, you wake up early and can't get back to sleep? Some kind of weird trick that your brain plays on you? I don't know. But in the morning, my eyes pop open at nine-thirty.

Rolling over to check my phone for messages, I groan. My room is just as depressingly bare as it was yesterday. Dang. I was sort of hoping everything had spontaneously moved itself back into place. Sure, it would have been borderline creepy, but I would have been too happy to care.

"This sucks," I mumble to myself. As I reach for my phone, my eyes fall on a framed photograph on the nightstand. It's a selfie of me and Sun on the beach in Virginia during spring break. Definitely not the best picture I've ever taken, but what selfie is? I just love the sun flashing off the waves behind us, and the stupid expressions we're both making. I had one printed for each of us and gave her a framed copy. No way I'm leaving this one behind.

Picking up the 5x7 frame, I head for the stack of boxes next to my desk. After a lot of effort, I'd managed to whittle down what I wanted to take with me to just one box. It's full almost to exploding, but I'll find a spot for this picture if it kills me. The boxes are all labeled, but I only had a ballpoint pen handy when I did it, so they're hard to read until I'm right next to them.

My handwriting still looks like a kid's loopy handwriting to me, and I wonder of eighteen is too late to master something more slanty and dignified. At least I don't dot my I's with hearts anymore.

Books to Keep

Books to Donate

Books to Take With

Not what I'm looking for.

I can't find the box labeled, *To Take*. There are

other boxes missing, too, like *Trash*, and *Shredding*.

One of my parents must have come in here after I finished and taken them out. My best guess is Ray. This is the sort of thing he does all the time — technically it's a favor, but part of me says he should have asked first.

I step into flip-flops to go down for breakfast and answers. Always best to have some kind of foot protection when my mom is in a purge and redecorate phase.

The hall smells faintly of paint, even though there are only three color samples painted on one wall. I swear she is single-handedly responsible for supporting at least half the latex paint industry. I'm surprised we can still fit between the walls considering how many layers my mother has put on the place. I bet if you measured it, she's actually decreased the square footage.

The new shade choices are all variants of bright yellow, so the walls almost vibrate with color. It's like a headache outside my head.

I'm still blinking away the after image when I get to the kitchen, which has mysteriously remained unscathed so far. Ray's in his usual spot at the kitchen table, reading the paper like there'll be a pop quiz later.

"'Mornin'," he says. "There's still some bacon on the counter."

"And I'm still a vegetarian."

Ray believes that repetition is the key to breaking me of this pesky vegetarianism. He never pushes, just…offers. Every. Single. Time.

"Just letting you know." He shakes out his paper and returns to memorizing box scores or whatever it is he's doing.

I pour myself a bowl of Grape Nuts and soy milk and take a seat at the table. Without speaking, Ray pushes the ads across the table to me. It's Back-to-School as far as the eye can see. The fact that a Bed Bath and Beyond ad is on top with "DORM LIFE" plastered on the cover makes me think my mother had a hand in creating this pile. The color-coordinated storage boxes remind me of my own room.

"Hey, Ray? Where did you put the boxes from my room?"

"Which ones are those?"

"I had that one for you to take to the shredder and there was one of trash, but what did you do with the other one?"

His bushy gray eyebrows pull together. "There were two in the stack that said Shredding on the cover. That's all I took."

My whole body goes still, like a rabbit who just spotted a dog. The Grape Nuts in my mouth suddenly weigh four times as much. With serious effort, I push the mass between my teeth and chew just enough to talk. "You took *two* boxes to the shredder?"

"The two in the stack," he says.

My heart plummets into my stomach and my knees go watery. "You took two boxes to the shredder?"

"The two in the stack...." he repeats, but he sounds a lot less certain.

"Are you sure?" The leaden mass of cereal makes its way toward my stomach, but not without a fight from my throat.

"Uh...."

Sweat prickles at my back and armpits. "Are you sure?" My pitch is a little shrieky and he flinches.

"I only took what you'd marked, I swear."

"Oh God."

"What's wrong?"

My eyes burn. "Are they still in the truck?"

"I took it all to the shredding place first thing this morning."

"Oh God." I stand up too quickly and my chair falls backwards. "Do you think they still have it?"

"What'd I do, Mara?"

"All my stuff...my yearbooks...pictures.... Oh God."

He's up from the table now, too. "Let's go."

———

A TENSE DRIVE LATER, a very cheerful guy at the commercial shredding facility informs us with absolute certainty that everything is shredded within six hours of drop-off unless otherwise designated.

My box was not otherwise designated. And they're running ahead of schedule this morning.

My high school career is pulp. Maybe someday it'll come back to me as a notebook, or the brown sleeve around a cup of coffee. Maybe toilet paper.

I never would have predicted the worst moment of my life would involve recycling.

The air dances with paper fiber, making my eyelashes work overtime in a blinking frenzy. My throat aches, but I can't tell if it's the result of yelling to be heard over the giant shredders ahead of me, or from the urge to cry. Probably both.

Mr. Cheerful gets considerably less cheerful when I start crying right there at the counter – as if I'm not pathetic enough showing up in my pajamas.

"Sorry, Miss." He does look sorry, but he also looks like he wants to get away from the sobbing girl across the counter. Me.

"Not your fault." Ray's fingers curl more tightly around my clavicle as he tries to guide me away from the desk. I step back until he puts his arm around my shoulders. "Come on, Sweetie, let me take you home."

I don't want to go. If I walk out of here, it's final. All my precious memories are gone. I stare at the desk guy, willing him to think of some other place my box might have gone. I need a miracle.

God, if you're listening, now would be the time to prove your existence. Is religious epiphany the sort of thing you can request?

I think my stare has crossed the line into psychotic territory, because the guy looks worried. "Listen kid, I feel bad about your box." He rummages in a drawer below the counter. "Here's a coupon. Up to five pounds free when you bring ten."

Is he kidding? He's not. My brain sends the message to my hand to take the coupon, but my hand resists for a few long seconds while the guy's getting more uncomfortable.

"Thanks," Ray says, taking the coupon and giving me a firmer direction with his hand on my arm. "Let's go, Mara."

My ears ring with the echo of the conveyors and

the shredders as we cross the parking lot to Ray's Ford F150. The black finish is coated in a fine layer of paper fiber.

"Man, this can't be good for our lungs, huh?" Ray forces a laugh.

The left side of my mouth smears up in a pathetic smile. I can tell it's not working from his double-take. I let my mouth drop and climb into the truck. The upholstery itches my thighs, so I slump down in the seat until the bottom of my polka-dotted pajama shorts are even with the edge of the seat. Now I can barely see out of the windshield, but there's nothing I want to see anyway. I want to wallow.

Ray turns the engine over and country music streams from the speakers. If I had any energy, I'd negotiate for a station change, but I don't care what's playing. In fact, the lyrics match my mood. Lost love, lonely nights, lonely days...that's about right.

Maybe I'm being dramatic, but it sure doesn't feel like it.

"You want to stop for ice cream?" My stepfather has been a firm believer in the healing power of ice cream for as long as I've known him. I have to admit, most of the time he's not wrong, but not even the amazing lemon-raspberry sorbet at Divino Gelato is going to make me feel better right now.

NEW STUDY SHOWS GELATO INEFFECTIVE AGAINST DEPRESSION, See Health, I think to myself.

"It's ten-thirty, Ray."

"Hey, when a young lady needs ice cream, time of day is not a factor."

Young lady? He gets weirdly formal and archaic when he's uncomfortable.

"I just want to go home."

He doesn't say anything for a while, drumming his fingers on the wheel. He turns the volume up a few times, then finally turns it down. "I'm so sorry, Mara."

"I know." I wipe my eyes. "It wasn't your fault." I have to say that, even though it would be really easy to blame him. I can't, not completely. I could have put the box outside my room. I should have kept it as far away as possible from my box of memories. I know the way Ray is – he's like a puppy in the body of a middle-aged man. Well-meaning, but likely to accidentally destroy your favorite shoes. What was I thinking?

When Ray pulls into the driveway, I see my mom already out in her garden. I ease out of the truck and push the door shut. Mom turns when she hears the thunk.

"Gone, huh?" She rocks back to sit on her heels.

"Gone." I nod, toeing up to the edge of the

driveway.

"Sorry, Mara." She rises to her feet, knees cracking and making her wince. She comes close to me but doesn't hug me with her dirty hands, instead propping the backs of her wrists awkwardly on her hips. "Was it just the yearbooks?"

I shake my head while tears line up for a chance to fall. Again. "All my pictures."

"Oh, Mar..." She can't resist momming me, even with dirty hands and gives me a hug that's all arms and wrists. It's enough to squeeze some more tears out of me, though.

"The negatives for all my 35 millimeter film were in there, too." I pull back to wipe my eyes again.

"At least we've got the prints that are framed in the hallway, right?"

"Yeah."

Incongruously, her expression brightens. "Your friends all have camera phones. There has never been a better documented generation of people in history, trust me. You'll get duplicates."

"We can get you one of those digital picture frames," Ray says.

"There you go," Mom agrees. "That would be better anyway. It won't take up so much room."

Ray is so uncomfortable, he's practically turning himself inside out. I know he would never do this on purpose, so I have to do something to let him off the hook. "Yeah... Thanks. That would be...nice."

They don't understand – it's all the little things that I can't get back. The ticket stub from my first concert, the poster from Sun's first show with her band, the keychain I got from Prom, every birthday card from the last four years.... It's all gone, too. And there aren't duplicates. But even worse than that are the originals from my photography classes. And all the negatives. What was I thinking putting the negatives in there?

I feel like my guts have been scooped out with a serving spoon. I'm a human jack-o-lantern.

"I'm gonna go call Sun. Tell her what happened."

"Okay." Mom checks the back of her hand for a clean spot before pressing it against my cheek. "It'll be okay, Mar. It's just stuff. You're still here."

Pressing my lips together, I manage to stifle my tears and keep from running as I go into the house. The smell of drying paint gives me an instant headache, and I long for the safety of my room, but it's such a mess right now, I know it's not going to be much of an improvement.

Maybe I'll just crawl into bed.

And pull the covers over my head.

And not come out until Christmas.

My phone, still abandoned on the pillow, vibrates with its reminder message. *Hey dummy, you didn't answer my last alert.* I turn it over to find a text from Sun.

All it says is: *Um, hello?! Are you dead?*

I turn my phone's camera on myself and snap a selfie of my tear-swollen face. It's truly awful. I send it to Sun: *Call me.*

The phone rings a moment later.

"Oh my God, what happened? Did someone actually die?" she says. "Did you stick your face in hornet's nest or something?"

"Worse." My voice cracks. "Ray accidentally took a box of my stuff to the shredder."

Her panicky tone drops. "Seriously? What'd you lose?"

I droop onto the pillows. "Everything."

"Wait, how many boxes was it?"

"Just one, but it had everything that mattered!"

"What are you talking about?"

"All the – " I gasp as a sob closes my throat. "Every – "

"Mariska, you're freaking out. Slow down."

"Every picture, cards, all my negatives...yearbooks." At least, that's what I mean to say, but I think it sounded more like, "Airy pig shur, cars, ama nay-gives...ear-boots"

"What?"

I take a shuddering breath and lock up my tears long enough to get something intelligible out. "It was everything I kept for the last four years. Concert tickets, yearbooks, cards...all my pictures. All of them."

"Oh...shit."

"Yeah."

"I'll be right there."

———

SUN WHISTLES WHEN she sees the carnage of my bedroom. "Whoa." She didn't come upstairs last night since I practically ran out the door when she got here.

I lift my arm off my eyes and have to blink away the extra Suns. "It's awful, isn't it?"

Her thin eyebrows head skyward. "You should consider majoring in Viking studies? 'Cause this is some quality pillaging you've done here."

A smile pulls the left side of my mouth back for a second. "I had to. You know my mom will."

"Mmm. I see what you mean."

Sun tiptoes around a laundry basket and a box of

sheets and perches on the end of my bed. She's got this peculiar way of perching, with her feet flat and her butt resting neatly above her heels, arms wrapped around her knees. It makes my own knees hurt just to watch her do it, but she never even flinches. "So, I thought it over."

"Yeah?"

"We can solve, like, half your problem."

I shift to face her, cross-legged, and pull Yanya, my decrepit teddy bear, onto my lap. At least he didn't meet a horrific, shredded end. The thought makes me shudder. "How?"

"One, we get pictures from everybody." She waits for me to nod. "Two, we go to the Riv and beg for replacement yearbooks." Another nod. "But I don't think there's much I can do about ticket stubs and cards and stuff."

I hadn't thought of going to school for the yearbooks. It's worth a try. "That's two thirds of my problem, not half."

"You're a nerd."

Shooting her a dirty look, I put Yanya to the side. "I guess it's better than nothing."

"It's better than half, if my high school math career wasn't entirely pointless."

I smile. "Okay, so I guess I should have said it's

better than half."

"You're damn right. Let's start workin' the phones."

I smile. "Thanks."

She gets her own phone from her messenger bag and starts tapping through screens. Before I realize her plan, she's snapped a picture of me.

"Hey!"

"I need proof of your pathetic-ness for this."

"I'm not pathetic."

"Oh you so are."

I'd love to protest, but I can still barely breathe through my nose and my cheeks are stiff with dried tears.

There's a soft knock on my door and my mom peeks in. "Mariska...oh, hey Sun, love the new hair."

"Thanks!" Sun grins. She and my mom are completely *sympatico* on the frequent color changing thing. Mom just prefers to change her walls rather than her hair.

"What was I...?" Mom's eyes tilt away in thought. "Right! Ray and I are heading out for a bit. He's feels so terrible about what happened. He's determined to get you one of those picture frames. Could you please try to pull yourself together for him?"

"Aww, poor old Ray," Sun says. "He's such a softie."

"Mara?"

I nod. "Yeah, I'll get it together."

"Good." She looks around the room. "I just can't get over how much better it looks in here. I got those paint samples. Maybe we could pick one out. Repaint. A fresh start. Would that make you feel better, sweetie?"

"Hey, Mom?"

"Hmm?"

"Can you please leave my room alone until I move out?"

"Oh fine." She scrapes her fingernail over a larger hole. "Two weeks, little friends. Then I'll throw you all a spackle party."

"Mom, you're talking to holes in the wall."

"They need my help, Mar."

I give her a flat look.

She laughs. "All right, all right. I'm going." With a wiggly-fingered wave, she's gone.

"Your mom is so weird." This is high praise from Sun.

"She has that look in her eyes." I inspect the wall beside the bed, where just yesterday my bulletin board hung, covered in pictures from Senior year. The awesome shot of the whole newspaper staff crammed into Mr. O'Neill's car. The one of all my friends on Halloween, dressed as the cast of *Rocky Horror Picture Show*. The

Decathlon team.

My chest feels tight. I rub my sternum with the heel of my hand. "Okay, let's do this."

"I'm on it." Sun taps out a message and hits SEND. "Now we wait. And you get dressed. We've got places to see, people to do."

[3]

YOU'D THINK WITH the number of people who have to be at a high school in the middle of August, it would be easier to find an open door. Then again, it is a Sunday. It takes us three attempts to find an open door, and it's not one of the usual student entrances.

Dust motes dance in the light slanting through the small, high window, jittering wildly when the door slams behind us and the detached hydraulic bangs against the wall. It has the distinct metallic slam of an institution, and I can't help jumping.

Sun laughs. "So much for stealth."

"Should we check in at the office or something?" I ask. Weird how you can feel like a stranger to a place after just a few months.

"Nah. Come on, let's go to the yearbook office."

"You think?"

"We could just steal them from the library if you're

feeling adventurous."

"It's probably locked, too."

She starts walking toward the main staircase. "Yearbook office it is. But for the record, I love that a locked door is the only reason you're not considering stealing them."

I smile a little. We stopped at Grind Me to get coffee drinks before we came to Arrow River, and the caffeine and sugar is doing me a world of good. It didn't do anything for my puffy face, but I'm definitely calmer.

We know the way well enough. The yearbook room is right next to the journalism room, where Sun and I probably spent more time in the last two years than anywhere else on the planet. But when I try the door, it's locked.

"Figures."

Sun stands on the toes of her wedges to peek through the window. "Yeah, definitely empty."

"See any yearbooks?" I can't help hoping.

"I don't see anything. It's wicked dark."

"Great."

"You think O'Neill's got a key to this room?"

"You think he's even here?" Mr. O'Neill is the faculty advisor for the student paper, and although he always kept long hours, I'm not sure he'll be here on a

Sunday during the summer.

Sun walks the few steps to the journalism office and tries the handle. The door pops open easily and she gives me a look of triumph.

The room is dim, except for the glow from three computer monitors, but it's easy to see the person sitting at one of the keyboards.

"Hello," I say, but the figure doesn't move. His back is turned to us. I squint as my eyes adjust to the weird blue-white glow of the screens. He still hasn't acknowledged us, but I'd recognize the curly mop of his hair anywhere. "Caine?"

Sun crosses the room and leans around him, until she finally invades his field of vision. He jumps, yelping and shoving back from the computer. The rolling chair slams into her and she staggers back, falling on her butt with a thud.

"Ow!" she hollers.

"Sun! Shit, I'm sorry!" He talks too loud, and I notice the earbuds in his ears.

"What the hell are *you* doing here?" Sun hitches onto one hip and makes a show of rubbing her backside. I offer her my hand.

"What are you guys doing here?" He's still talking too loud.

"Are you okay?" I ask Sun.

She frowns. "Yeah, I'm fine. I'm gonna have a nasty bruise but *I'm fine*!" She raises her voice for the last part so Caine can hear her.

"You okay?" he shouts.

I roll my eyes and give his earphones a yank. They drop to his lap and we can hear the distant report of his music – way too loud.

"You okay?" he repeats.

"Yeah, no thanks to you." Sun staggers to her feet with my assistance.

"You scared the crap out of me."

"If you didn't have your music cranked to Hearing Damage, maybe we wouldn't have scared you." I point to my ear.

He gives me a *Yeah, yeah* eye roll. "Seriously, what are you guys doing here?"

I've heard the story from Sun enough times today that it seems like it happened to someone else, so I feel okay telling it myself. Caine squints at me while I'm talking, but otherwise doesn't react.

"We're on a mission for yearbooks," Sun concludes. "But the office is locked."

"No shit, nobody's crazy enough to be here right now." Caine pushes his glasses up. "Well, except me, I guess."

"What *are* you doing here?" I ask.

He digs his fingers into his sproingy nest of curly hair, yanking it away from his face for a second. It's his signature gesture, and seeing it takes me instantly to every newspaper meeting we had during his reign as editor-in-chief, and countless hours spent studying for the Academic Decathlon.

"Caitlin got mono." He sighs. "Who gets freaking mono in August?"

"So how is this your problem?"

"O'Neill." Caine sighs again. "There was begging."

"Please. You know you jumped at the chance to get back in the saddle." Sun thumps the back of his chair.

"Yeah, who wouldn't jump at the chance to piece together the Welcome Back edition of *The Arrow River Chronicle*?" He leans back in his chair. "I love copyediting articles written by people who just finished sophomore English."

"And yet you're here..." I raise my eyebrows.

"There was begging. You look awful, by the way, Mariska."

"Thank you."

Sun interrupts, "Is O'Neill around here anywhere?"

"Nope." Caine shakes his head.

"Damn. I was hoping he'd have keys to the yearbook office." She boosts herself to sit on one of the thick metal work tables.

"You can check if you want." Caine digs in the pocket of his cargo shorts and produces a heavy ring of keys.

"You've got the keys?" Sun's wooden heels clunk against the table leg. Her eyes go wide with possibilities.

"Yep." He holds them out to me. "I don't know if any of them will open your door, but go for it."

"Thank you so much!" I snatch them and dash out of the room. The empty halls echo with the sound of jangling metal as I try key after key after key, but none of them release the lock.

Damn it.

"Let me try." Sun has followed me down the hall and she repeats the fruitless cycle from the first key to the last. "Oh come on, O'Neill!" she bitches.

"You need to try all the keys two more times. And hop on one foot while singing the Barney theme song in German." Caine calls from the door of the journalism office.

"Hardy-har-har." Sun pitches the keys to him.

"Never!" I gasp. "You know not to speak of that purple devil in front of me!"

"*I love you...you love me...*" he sings softly.

"You promised!" I fake a quivering lip and cover my ears.

"You're right, I'm sorry." He holds out both hands in supplication. "We made a lot of promises that night."

"Oh good Lord, are you two done yet?" Sun props her hands on her hips. She has never enjoyed imaginary one-ups. But then, she wasn't on the Decathlon team, and that's where we started playing, though none of us would admit there's actually a game at work.

I turn to her. "Yeah, sorry. What's up?"

"Look, there's no yearbooks here, and I can't stand the flatness of my hair much longer, so can we go?"

Caine shakes his head in disbelief. "You're telling me you don't want to stick around and help me put this issue to bed? For old time's sake?"

For just a moment, I do want to stay. The newspaper was my thing. My niche at school. Working late hours after school, the weight of my camera around my neck at every school event, listening to Mr. O'Neill tell stories about the faculty lunch room. On the day we finished our last issue as seniors, I felt like a little part of me got left behind in this room. I'd like to keep taking pictures for the newspaper in college, but there's no guarantee. Here in the journalism office, I feel like myself.

It's tempting to stay, though I'm sure he doesn't need a photographer. All of that will be done already.

"Yeah, no thanks." Sun wrinkles her nose. "I wouldn't even be in the building if it weren't for The Shredding." Her tone implies the capital letters on the last two words.

"I should go," I agree.

"Suit yourself." Caine shrugs.

"Just slap the issue together and get the hell out of here," Sun says.

"Yeah, I know, but..." He shrugs again.

"You can't." I understand. He doesn't want his name on something half-assed. He takes the newspaper very seriously. You don't become Editor-in-Chief as a hobby. I didn't graduate fourth in the class because I hate school.

"I can't." Suddenly, his face brightens. "Hey, are you guys coming to the meeting tomorrow?"

"What meeting?" I ask.

"For the new staffers. Don't you remember last summer when we met for the first time? Beckett, Kim, and Irene were there?"

Then I do remember. Every summer Mr. O'Neill tries to get the recent graduates to come back and sit in on the first meeting with the new newspaper staff for the preschool planning meeting. They've got the Welcome Back issue to get out, and there's too much work to get it done after classes have officially started.

"I was definitely not planning on it," Sun says.

"I forgot about it," I admit. The e-mail from O'Neill seems a lifetime ago.

"But now that you remember, you're going to come," Caine says, like it's not up for discussion.

"We'll be there," I say.

Sun makes a sound somewhere on the border between gasp and cluck. "We?"

"Thank you."

"We?" Sun repeats.

"It's not like he's asking us to hide a body, Sun," I say.

"Seriously," he says. "Besides, I always do that myself."

I nod. "No witnesses."

He taps two fingers at his temple, then swings his fingers between us to indicate we're on the same wavelength. I smile.

Meanwhile, Sun is doing a full body pout, complete with a groaning-whining hybrid and some serious clomping of her sandals. "Ohhhhhh, fiiiiiinnnne," she drawls.

"Molding young minds, Sun. This is the Lord's work." Caine presses his palms together beneath his chin and looks heavenward.

"A liar and a blasphemer. Impressive," I say.

Sun just rolls her eyes. "All right then, Citizen Caine. We're outta here."

"See you tomorrow," he calls after us as we head for the exit.

"You owe me big time," Sun mutters.

"You are the greatest best friend in the history of the world."

"Damn right."

[4]

HOURS LATER, Mom is inspecting color swatches under various lights in the living room when I enter. Ray's in the room too, but his attention is clearly more on the local news which is humming from the TV in the center of the room. Everything is pulled away from the walls in preparation for my mother's latest color whim.

"How you doin', Mara?" Mom says when she sees me.

"I'm...okay."

Ray snaps to attention. "I got you something!" He hurries out of the room.

"He's just a mess over this whole thing," Mom whispers to me.

"Top of the line." Ray is back before I can respond, holding out a yellow and white box for me. "They tell me this is the one you gotta have." He gives the box an enthusiastic tap.

"Thanks, Ray." I take it from him and step in for a

hug. He seems surprised, thumping me on the back a little harder than necessary.

"I'm just – aw, shit, Mariska, I'm just so sorry."

"Ray." My mom rolls her eyes at him.

"It's okay. I know you didn't do it on purpose."

"Well..." he prompts, shooing me with his hands. "Are you gonna get it set up or what?"

Actually, I was planning to do some pretty intense wallowing this evening, if truth be told. I have to work tomorrow, and being a nanny to eight-year-old twin girls doesn't give me much time for self-pity. I figure I deserve a little quality feeling-sorry-for-myself time. But now, looking at Ray's I-have-to-make-this-right eagerness, I can't say no.

"Right now," I say, pasting on a smile. I can tell from his reaction it's a much better smile than the scary one I gave him at the recycling center. I'm either getting better at this, or I'm actually feeling less despondent. If I had to guess, I'd say it's the latter.

Up in my disaster area of a bedroom, I start opening all the files I've gotten from my friends today. The sheer magnitude of the project hits me when I see the files number over 1,000. I know there are going to be duplicates--it's not like my friends haven't given me pictures via e-mail and Facebook for the last four years--

but there's also a lot of new stuff.

I should have had another coffee.

But by the time I've got the last of them cropped, adjusted, and transferred to the frame, it's pitch black outside and my eyes are burning from staring at the screen too long. At least they're too scorched to cry now.

My mom and Sun were right about being able to replace most of the pictures. I'm almost drowning in them, in fact. I didn't even put most of them on the frame, or I would have been looking at four hundred pictures of my spring break trip to Virginia Beach before I saw anything else. I've never been so happy about digital photography in my life.

Actually, I've never really been happy about digital photography at all in my life.

I got my first film camera from my grandmother when I was eight and I was instantly hooked. Then I discovered film processing and it was destined to be a life-long love affair. I love the effort it takes to capture a beautiful photograph without the safety net of Photoshop. I love the heavy quiet of the dark room, when the red light can just barely keep the blackness at bay and the dark feels like a living thing leaning on you. I love holding prints in my hands.

Most of my best print work is framed and propped

against the vibrating yellow walls of my mother's hallway, awaiting rehanging, so at least I didn't lose those. Although they are now the only copies that will ever exist. Like an idiot, I put my negatives in the same box. All to protect my precious things from one of my mom's purges.

IRONY CONTINUES TO BE A BITCH, See Op-Ed.

I rub my eyes while the photo frame goes through its weirdly long boot cycle. I probably overloaded it and it's going to start smoking.

But no, after ninety seconds — which equals ninety minutes in anxiety time — it flashes to life with a photo of some people from the Academic Decathlon Team. It's a familiar scene; I remember my version of the photo perfectly. But the sensation reminds me of going to a different grocery store than usual and finding the cereal aisle on the back wall when it should be in the middle like always. Whoever took the picture was standing at least ten feet to my left when I took one with my camera.

The frame fits on my nightstand with a little shuffling, and I find I can watch the frame change if I lay just right on my side. This might be like watching my own funeral. All these memories, not quite as I remember them. I can't stop staring.

Some pictures trigger memories of other events

and my mind expects them to come next in the sequence, but it's all randomized. The chaos is a bit dizzying, though I have to confess it's exciting too. In a really lame, yay-it's-ravioli-day-in-the-cafeteria way.

On my second trip down this bumpy memory lane, I become aware of the potholes. Some photos came from my camera and mine alone. Those are really, truly gone. The thought of going on without them brings tears to my eyes yet again.

There are plenty of things I'll never get back. That hurts, but not nearly as much as some of my photographs.

I am the memory-keeper among my friends. The one who can always be counted on to catch the unexpected moments. Sure, everybody has a camera phone, but somehow I always seemed to be the one with my finger on the shutter.

I feel like I've let down all of my friends, too.

Gone: the photo of the paper staff in Mr. O'Neill's car. All of us crammed inside like sardines.

Gone: the prints and the negatives from the day I took pictures of Sun in her traditional Korean *hanbok*.

Gone: the picture of my best girlfriends at sunrise in Virginia Beach.

And there's one photo I'll never see again, no matter what: the only picture of my biological father.

Gone, gone, gone.

I can't let myself fall asleep yet. What if I forget these missing pieces while I'm sleeping? I scoot out of bed and find a pen and paper. I have to write down these moments before they escape from my mind forever. The photos were the only evidence they ever happened in the first place. I owe it to myself to get them on paper. I owe it to my friends. I owe it to my father.

Already I worry I've missed something. What if I've already forgotten something important? What if I never remember it?

The list is short. Just seven items.

1. Newspaper staff in O'Neill's car.

2. Sun in her hanbok.

3. Sunrise in Virginia Beach.

4. Prom.

5. Clown soccer.

6. The Drive-In series.

7. My father.

Too short. Surely, I missed something. How can only seven pictures feel like such a huge percentage of my life?

I guess maybe I have time for that wallowing in

self-pity I'd planned on after all.

[5]

I CALL SUN five times to make sure she's going to show up for the newspaper meeting tonight, but she's either trapped under something heavy, or ignoring me. Either one is concerning, though the latter is certainly more annoying.

Nannying for the twins normally makes the day fly by, but this one drags as I haul my phone out for a spot check every thirty seconds.

Of course Olivia and Madeline have a sixth sense for when my brain is not on them, so they spend the day peppering me with questions and asking to do all my least favorite things. I would have sworn they outgrew *Pretty Pretty Princess* two years ago, but they demand to play.

Thankfully, Mrs. LaPierre gets home a little early, so I'm relieved of duty in enough time to book it over to the high school. I'm hoping to get there a few minutes early for the meeting, while the front office is still open. There are cars scattered in the faculty lot this time, and I think I've got a shot at finding someone with the authority to give me yearbooks.

I'm in luck. The school secretary is ensconced behind her desk, as if it's September, only she's wearing denim shorts and a t-shirt with a reddish stain on the front. Ketchup? I hope it's ketchup.

She smiles at me when I walk in, but it's not a smile of recognition. I guess I'm not surprised; I didn't have much cause to come to the office while I was a student here. Honor students are practically mythical creatures to the administration – they've all heard of us, but they've never seen most of us. When I give her my name, though, she nods in recognition.

"I always loved your name." She smiles. "Very artistic sounding."

Very Hungarian sounding. Goes with my very Hungarian-looking nose and my big ears. She doesn't care about my self-consciousness though, so I just say, "Thank you."

I explain what I'm here for, and she makes one of those oh-gosh-I'd-love-to-help-you-but... faces. "Oh dear. You lost all four?"

"Are there any extra copies?"

"You may be able to order a second copy." She turns away from me to dig in a file drawer for the appropriate form. "Ah. Here we go. Now, I'm not completely sure you'll be able to get the old ones. Maybe only last year's."

I take the form and go weak in the knees. "Seventy-five dollars? Each?"

"I think there's some handling fees as well." She stands and tries to read the form upside down. "Well, you'll have to check the fine print. I can't see it from here."

Great. Three hundred dollars, plus fees. I knew they were expensive, but I didn't really think about it when my parents were signing the checks. I don't have that kind of cash to spare and my mom isn't going to lend me three hundred bucks to get back a bunch of yearbooks. She probably used hers for kindling years ago. There's definitely no way they've survived twenty years of her purging fits.

"Are you all right?" the secretary asks.

Pinching my lips together, I force myself to stay calm. "Do you know if anyone is in the yearbook office?"

"No idea. You're welcome to go check yourself." Her face brightens as she seizes on a way to help me, no matter how small.

I thank her and push the glass doors open. The heat of the hall hits me as soon as I'm outside the air-conditioned oasis of the administration offices. I might as well try my luck at the yearbook room again. Who knows?

Maybe someone is there looking for a way to dispose of all the unclaimed copies from the last four years.

Stranger things have happened.

I have to super-spy my way past the open door of the journalism room to get to the yearbook office. I can hear voices in there already and I don't want to get sucked into the meeting until I've made an attempt to get my yearbooks. But the door is locked, just like yesterday.

Of course.

I slump against the locked door and let a couple of frustrated tears sneak past my squeezed lids. Why is every force in the universe conspiring against me with these damn yearbooks? Maybe Sun is onto something with her library heist idea. I should have checked O'Neill's keys for one to open the library when I had the chance.

Forcing a breath, I flick my knuckles beneath my eyes to clear away any tears. I'm here for the meeting, after all, and going in there crying is not the impression I want to give.

Okay, I'm under control. I lift my chin and go into the J-room.

Mr. O'Neill is there, with a couple of soon-to-be-seniors, and all of them are bent over a printout of something. O'Neill sees me and gives me a nod without interrupting the flow of whatever instructions he's giving the others.

Caine is sitting at the same computer as yesterday, with his earbuds blocking out the rest of the world. I don't know how he thinks about editing with music blasting in his ears like that. I always end up typing in song lyrics when I try to listen to music while I write papers.

Rather than risk getting knocked to the floor like Sun did yesterday, I make a wide circle around him so he can catch me in his peripheral vision. Still, he jumps a little, but flicks his earbuds free and says, "Hey. You showed up."

"I told you I would."

"And Sun?" He twists to look toward the door.

"Possibly trapped under something heavy."

He nods. "Refrigerator?"

"I think a polar bear is more likely."

"Dead polar bear or alive?"

"Hard to say with Sun." I shrug, then indicate the computer monitor. "How's it going?"

"Almost done." He slips his glasses off to scrub the computer burn away from his eyes. "How's your picture quest going?"

"Not bad. Still no yearbooks."

"Nobody's there?"

"Locked. But apparently they'll find a key if I come

up with three hundred bucks." He looks confused, so I explain about reordering.

"I presume you're not crazy enough to shell out the cash?" He adjusts his glasses on the bridge of his nose a few times before he seems satisfied.

"It's more that I'm not rich enough."

Pushing back from the desk, he asks, "Why do you even want those things?"

My body goes stiff on reflex. "Why wouldn't I?"

He does his hair shoving move. "They're just yearbooks. It's just high school."

"What's wrong with high school?"

"It's like four years of sitting in the waiting room at the dentist." He makes a face. "You just rush through it to start your real life."

I look at him like an alien just burst out of his stomach. "You don't actually think that do you?"

He doesn't answer.

"Then why bother with the paper? The Decathlon team? You were Salutatorian, for God's sake. What's the point of that if this is just a giant dentist's waiting room?"

"You need something to keep you busy while you wait, right?"

"So high school is just a giant issue of *Highlights* magazine to you?"

His lips curve into an almost-smile. "I like that."

"I wasn't trying to amuse you."

"Mariska, come on. You don't even care about ninety percent of the people in our class, do you? You probably don't even like most of them."

I open my mouth on a protest, but right away I realize he's probably underestimating. It's more like ninety-five — maybe even ninety-nine — percent. But the ones I do care about mean the world to me. Lips pressed together, I glare at him. "Are you telling me there's not a single person you'd like to remember from the last four years of your life?"

"I didn't say that."

"Sure sounded like it."

"High school was fine. Some good stuff happened. But I already remember the good stuff. I don't need a book full of pictures of people I don't even like to remember all the other stuff I don't even want to remember." His eyebrows pull together as he thinks through his last sentence, then he nods.

"Yeah, you say that now. What about in ten years when you can't remember my name?"

"I think it's fair to say no one will ever forget your name, Mariska Bokori."

"It was an example."

"I haven't forgotten anyone so far." He shrugs.

I shake my head. "If it means so little to you, why are you even here right now?"

"I didn't say it didn't mean anything to me. I just don't need a yearbook to remember high school." He drums his fingers on the work table. "Besides, there's plenty I'd just as soon forget."

"Bah humbug."

He smirks. "Okay, fine. But, please, promise me you won't spend three-hundred bucks on a picture book of idiots."

"Caine, I had no idea you were so misanthropic." I cross my arms and raise my eyebrows.

Scowling but amused, he flicks a handy paperclip at me. "I'm downright philanthropic and I'll prove it to you."

"Oh?"

"You can have my yearbooks. All four years."

My eyebrows go sky high. "You're kidding."

"Nope. They're yours."

"I don't have three hundred dollars." My heart is racing at the thought of my goal being so close.

He shakes his head. "I don't want your money."

"What *do* you want?"

He shakes his head. "Nothing. You just have to

pick them up."

"You've got to be kidding me."

"I would never lie to you about ditching my unwanted yearbooks." He lays a hand over his heart. "Trust me, Mariska, this is a win-win situation. You want 'em, I don't."

I purse my lips and consider the offer. "I'm pretty sure you're going to regret this at some point in the future, but I really want them, so I'm going to take the chance." I hold out my hand to seal our gentlemen's agreement.

"You got a deal." We shake on it.

"All right, I'm here, are you happy?" Sun's voice makes us both turn to the door.

"I thought I got rid of you," Mr. O'Neill teases.

"Never. If I died today, I'd haunt you, O'Neill." Sun's hair is restored to its usual corona of carefully planned disorder.

O'Neill shakes his head. "All right, people, let's get this meeting going."

The meeting is actually kind of fun. It's comfortable and familiar, like slipping on my favorite pair of jeans. I get to talk to Mick, the upcoming staff photographer, who is not only hilarious but totally sympathetic when I tell him about my lost pictures. He was a junior last year, so he remembers the picture we all took in Mr. O'Neill's precious Chevy Camaro.

"Oh man, I thought his head was going to explode when we started climbing in there." Mr. O'Neill loves his Camaro like some people love their children. He even parks it in the rear of the faculty lot straddling two spaces so no one can park next to it.

We'd been waiting for him to arrive last September for a Saturday meeting, and he was late...

...We all knew where he'd park, so we sat around in the back of the faculty lot, ready to pounce. All we wanted to do was harass him for being late, when we'd all agreed to come into school on a Saturday and stuff papers. They'd been delivered late by the printer and in order get the issue out on Monday, we had to do it on the weekend.

As soon as the throaty rumble of the Camaro announced his arrival, we all stood and gave him our best impatient looks. A few people tapped their wrists as he rolled closer.

"Yeah, yeah, I'm late. Sorry guys. Now back up." He had the two roof segments off the car, so it was easy to hear him and see him flick his hand at us.

"You know what I want to do?" Sun announced. "I want to touch the Camaro."

"Don't even think about it, McInerney."

"My hands are clean," she said, holding them up as evidence. "I won't hurt it."

Everyone was crowding closer now, threatening the red car with wiggling pointer fingers.

It was Mick who did it first, tapping the finish lightly on the corner of the trunk. "Woo-ee! Now I can die happy!" he hollered.

"Ha ha, you've all had your fun," Mr. O'Neill said. "Now scatter."

We backed up, letting him pull into the space – two spaces – he wanted, but then we were on him like a swarm.

"Can I sit in it?" Sun asked.

"No."

"Oh come on! It'll be fun!" She let her fingertips dance lightly on the black interior of the door. Not touching the cherry finish, but still touching the car.

O'Neill could always be counted on to rise to the occasion. He cultivated his curmudgeonly persona like my mother and her lilies. "You wouldn't...."

In a flash, Sun had the door open and was sitting in the passenger seat. She cackled wildly. "I wish you could see your face!"

It all went quickly from there. Soon the entire staff was crammed into the spaces made by the t-top, smashed together like flowers in a bouquet. Of course I had my camera, and O'Neill, after some serious fussing for show, took the picture.

He swore up and down he'd never forgive us, and that he would take a restraining order out against us on his car's behalf, but he didn't, of course. And for almost a year, the picture hung on my bulletin board, making me laugh every time I remembered.

———————

WHEN THE FIRST glimmer of the idea comes to me, I have to press two fingers to my lips to hold in a giggle. It's insane. But I lose track of what Mr. O'Neill is saying because I can't stop thinking about it.

Maybe it's not insane.

I decide to test it on Sun. Poking her to get her attention, I whisper, "How pissed do you think O'Neill would get if we all got in his car again to take a new picture?"

She grins. "Pissed. It would be hilarious."

We go quiet for a few more minutes while the meeting continues, but I can tell she's into the idea. She pulls her feet onto her chair to perch in her favorite, knee-mauling crouch. If I know my Sun-ology, the pose signifies pent up energy.

As soon as the meeting is over, Sun unfurls herself

to stand on her chair. "You guys, Mariska needs our help."
She tells my story one more time. I have to admit, her flair
for the dramatic really helps make it seem tragic. I feel
sorry for me.

LOCAL GIRL IS MOST PATHETIC IN
COUNTRY, See Society.

Mr. O'Neill claps me on the shoulder, almost
taking me off my feet with the force of it. I've always
suspected he's so firm with us to avoid any accusations
about inappropriate behavior. I guess maybe if I were a
teacher, I'd feel the same way.

He gives my deltoid a squeeze. "I'm sorry about
you losing everything."

"Thanks."

"I know it's probably not something you're missing,
but you're welcome to come into the J-room and get copies
of any of your photos. Old issues." He shrugs.

Instantly, I feel the newsprint between my fingers
and smell the basementy smell of the darkroom. "That
would be really nice." Then, I remember. "Do you have
access to the yearbook room? I was hoping there might be
some extra copies."

He shakes his head. "Nope, sorry kiddo. But if
there's anything else I can do for you, just let me know."

"Actually..." Sun's been eavesdropping and now

she swoops in.

"Not you, McInerney."

"This is for Mariska."

O'Neill narrows his eyes at us. "What?"

EVERY SINGLE PERSON agrees to be in the picture. A chance to tread on O'Neill's precious upholstery is just too much, I guess. Whatever the reason, I'm damn near dancing as we troop out the side entrance to the faculty lot.

"How long is this going to take?" a junior — senior now, I guess – named Tim asks. "I have to be home at six." He glances at his watch.

"Oh, not long. Right, Mr. O'Neill?" Sun grins. She's enjoying this on a whole different level than me.

"I can't believe I'm letting you heathens do this again," he mutters.

Mick says, "We just want to help out Mariska."

"Personally I'm in it for the chance to leave a big ol' footprint on the leather," Ruthie says. "Maybe I'll even rub my bare toes on the windshield."

"You do have your camera, Bokori?" Mr. O'Neill asks.

"Of course." I reach for my backpack, slung on one

shoulder. Caine, walking behind me, has to jump out of the way. His expression is neutral, which in itself is pretty telling. Everyone else is bubbling with excitement.

"You think this is stupid, don't you?" I ask.

"No." But his tone says that's not exactly true. "Unnecessary, maybe."

"Does that mean you won't be in the picture?"

He pushes his glasses up. "I'm not soulless."

I smile and thread my arm through his for a squeeze. "Yay! Thank you." He leans into it for a second, then backs away.

"Keys!" Deanne bellows as we reach the Camaro.

"I must be nuts," O'Neill sighs.

"Oh come on, you know you missed us," Sun says.

He snorts, but smiles.

"Thanks for doing this," I say.

"For letting you defile my upholstery again, you mean?" he asks.

"Yep." Sun mimes thumbing a key fob. "Let us in!"

"Pushy, pushy." He reaches into his pocket and we all hear the thunk of the locks opening.

"Let's do this!" someone shouts.

Everyone starts pressing into the car before the T-top panels are even off. I pause to put my backpack on the ground and dig out my camera. From the car, all I can hear are groans and giggles.

"Oh my God, it's hot as fuck in here!"

"Watch the hair!"

"Ow! That was my hand!"

"Sorry!"

"Holy crap!"

"Whose elbow is in my back?!"

Everyone else is already crammed into the car when I give Mr. O'Neill my new DSLR Canon, my graduation gift from my parents.

I start to show O'Neill how it works, but he waves me off. "I know how to use a camera, Bokori. Go get in there before someone suffocates."

The T-top is open and already filled beyond capacity. Caine stands back, surveying the limited space remaining.

"Are we ready?" a female voice squeaks from the other side of the car.

"Not yet!" I say.

"How the hell are we going to do this?" Caine asks.

"There were two more people last time and we did it." There were fourteen staffers last year, and somehow we all managed it, though I was in the car a lot earlier last time around. It seems impossible now.

Caine tilts his head. "After you."

"All right." I wipe my palms on my shorts. "I'm coming in!"

I can't even tell what body parts I'm using as handholds to climb in, much less who they belong to, as I squeeze my way into invisible spaces. It's oppressively hot in the car, even with most of the roof gone. It's the kind of parking lot heat that makes my face break out in sweat after five seconds. The bodies of my friends are giving off even more heat.

TWELVE LOCAL TEENS DIE IN PARKED CAR, See Headlines.

I start to wobble and have to grab blindly at whatever I can reach. Someone I'm clutching twitches wildly, laughing, though the sound is displaced to the other side of the car. Everyone is moving, squirming, and laughing. My center of gravity shifts and reshapes as people scramble for purchase on other sweaty bodies.

I'm not even stable when I feel someone's hand on my thigh. It's got to be Caine; he's the only one left. Pushing just a little harder, I find a handhold and manage to get myself locked into position. Or as much as I'm going to get anyway.

"Are we ready yet?" The same voice as before asks, and I recognize it as Deanne now that I'm closer.

"Almost," I tell her.

"You better frickin' appreciate this, Mariska!" Mick says, then makes an unintelligible sound. "Stop it!" he howls. "No tickling!"

Someone next to me groans, bodies shift against me and someone's hand scrabbles across my butt looking for anything to grip. It's gone in a millisecond, but I can't help laughing.

"Someone just grabbed my butt!" I announce.

"Sorry," Caine grunts. "I was falling."

Sun whoops, "Woo hoo!" and someone else whistles.

Then I get an elbow in the back, and with a final shove, Caine is next to me. "We're good, let's get this done," he says.

"Take the picture!" Deanne yowls.

"You guys are idiots," O'Neill says, but he's already got my camera raised.

"Everybody say 'Cheese,'" someone instructs.

"Say, 'William Randolph Hearst!'" O'Neill corrects.

We all laugh and he takes the picture before anyone says anything else.

"One more!" I shout because I don't trust anyone to take a good picture.

He complies, then gives us a thumbs up.

"Get me out of here!" Deanne says.

At once, the mass of bodies begins to undulate even more than before. Someone pushes me abruptly and I smack my head into Caine's jaw.

"Sorry!"

"Ow. At least we're even now."

Somehow the car begins to empty. Even though I was second last to get in, I'm nowhere near the first to get out. At last, the twelve of us stand on the blacktop, disheveled, sweating, and breathing hard.

"I feel like I just got out of the world's lamest orgy." Mick plucks the neck of his t-shirt away from his body.

"I'm pretty sure I got unintentionally molested," Sun says cheerfully.

"By who?"

She shrugs. "Who knows? But I'm pretty sure I unintentionally molested a few people, too."

"Thanks, everybody," I say. "Really. You don't know what it means to me that you did this."

"I better get a copy this time," Deanne says.

"And keep the originals somewhere safe," Mick adds.

Sun catches my eye and raises her eyebrows as if to say, *Well?* I close the distance between us and wrap her in a sweaty hug. "Thanks for being pushy."

"I know it's not the same picture..."

"No, no. It's great. Really."

She shrugs. "Hey, we got one back anyway, right?"

"I've never been so sweaty in my life." Deanne says, flapping the bottom of her shirt. "I'm not even sure it's all mine."

"Sorry."

She smiles. "You know what? It was kind of fun."

A tap on my shoulder makes me turn. Mr. O'Neill holds out my camera. "There you go, kid."

"Thank you so much, Mr. O'Neill."

"Just don't tell anyone, huh? I'm never doing this again."

"You got it. Am I still allowed to pick through the negatives in the J-room?"

He tells me that I am, and gives me his hours for the rest of the week. Then he gives the group a wave. "You guys are nuts. Have a good one."

"Thanks again, Mr. O'Neill!" Sun shouts after him.

I check the display on the camera. That's one thing I have to give to digital – at least I can see the fruits of Mr. O'Neill's labor right away. The glare from the evening sun makes it hard to tell for sure, but I think he got a good shot. Definitely not the same shot as the one I lost, but a good shot. It makes me smile.

"Happy?" Sun asks.

A lump forms in my throat, so I just nod.

"Good."

And the it hits me. It hits me so hard I actually get a pain in my head. I can do this with the rest of the pictures. It won't be perfect, but at least it would be something. Something I can actually do about this mess. My hands start to jitter over the camera's buttons, just for something to do. I take two steps forward, stop short and tip back on my heels so far I start to lose my balance.

"What's your short circuit?" Deanne asks.

"I just had an idea."

"Ding!" Sun holds an imaginary light bulb above her head.

"I can do this with all the other missing photos." My heart is in my throat. "We can do this. That is, if you guys will help me."

"How many photos are you talking about?" Deanne asks.

"Six. Well, five now." None of them can help get back the picture of my father, so I mentally leave it off the list.

"That's not so bad." She shrugs. "Yeah, I'd help."

Sun purses her lips. "It might be a little more complicated than you're thinking." She's already seen the list. And she's right.

But I don't care how hard it is. This is something I can actually do for myself. A real solution. I have to do this. I look at my best friend and will her to help me. Clasped hands, puppy dog eyes, lips silently forming the word, Please!

"Oh stop, you know I'm in," Sun says. "Hell, it was practically my idea."

"Yay!" I can't restrain myself from bouncing and clapping. "We've got planning to do."

[6]

THE TWINS CAN'T stop staring at Sun when she meets us at the park the next day. I can hardly stop staring myself. It's been a long time since I saw her in her traditional Korean hanbok.

Not long before we met, Sun and her very white, very Irish adoptive parents visited her native Korea for the first time since she was a year old. She'd brought the traditional clothing home with her and mostly, it lives in the back of her closet. She put it on for me the first time I slept over at her house, when we were fourteen, and I took a picture of her. It's one of the best pictures I ever took, though I can't understand why. I was just getting interested in photography at that point and the composition was nothing but chance.

When I see her bright blue skirt and red jacket, I can't wait to get another shot at capturing her on film.

"You look amazing!" I untangle my legs from the picnic table where we've set up camp, and run to throw my arms around her.

"I know, right?" Sun looks down at her brilliant skirt. "I haven't worn this thing in ages."

Liv and Maddy are gaping at my best friend.

"Hey girls," she says. "You like my outfit?"

Liv nods slowly, and Maddy doesn't move at all. "You look like Mulan," Liv says.

Sun frowns. "I do not. She's Chinese. I am Korean."

Maddy elbows Liv in admonition and Liv returns it with a scowl.

"You ready for the picture?" I ask.

"Let me just put my headpiece on." She hauls up the long skirt, revealing plaid golf-style pants cut off to knee length underneath. I have to laugh at the black combat boots. I know she has the traditional Korean shoes that go with this outfit, but the narrow fit and upturned toes are not her favorite thing. From her pocket, she pulls out a wide red band of silk that goes around her head and a handful of bobby pins to get her hair back.

While she works, I notice she has on very soft, traditional make-up. So unlike her usual charcoal eyes and wine-colored lipsticks.

When the headpiece is on, I hardly recognize her. She looks like an exotic princess, albeit with fire-engine red hair. The bright sunlight of the August day seems to make her clothing glow. The saturation on this photo is going to be key. I can't wait to see them full-screen.

Maddy and Liv run ahead of us as we head for a clear spot. I don't want any playground equipment in the background.

"So I might have a lead on a place to go dancing for the prom thing," Sun says as we stroll.

"Yeah?" For the group prom picture, we're planning a night out with everyone in their formal dresses and suits. Might as well go dancing in fancy clothes, right?

"You know that guy Miguel, who was in that awful band at that one show?" She waits for me to nod. "Apparently he goes dancing with some people from his ethnic dance troupe to this place called The Blue Canary. It's like an old-school supper club and they have dances on Saturday nights."

"That sounds perfect!"

"He says there will probably be a lot of old people there."

I chew on the inside of my cheek, while up ahead, Liv is attempting back walkovers. Maddy settles for cartwheels. "Careful girls!" I call when they get too close to a tree. "I think that's okay, don't you?" I ask Sun.

"The old people?" she asks. "Hell yeah. I think it's

awesome."

I laugh. "All right. So Prom Part Two is going down at the Blue Canary."

"Sweet." Sun lets her skirt drop from one hand to give me a high five. "We gotta work on that name though."

"How about here?" Maddy bellows from about fifty feet ahead. She sticks her arms out Vanna White style to indicate a lovely weeping willow.

I give her a thumbs up and smile at Sun. "You're on."

She gathers up her skirt again and runs ahead to the spot the girls scouted. I circle for a bit, looking for the best angle for the sunlight before settling onto my knees in my favorite stance for stillness.

Sun takes up a traditional pose, with her hands clasped under the long tails of the jacket. She tips her chin down and gives me a soft smile. It's so not Sun, but she's doing a great job.

I get a couple of good shots while she maintains a calm face. The display on my camera shows me that I captured a very suitable imitation of the original shot, which was done in Sun's backyard, but something seems...wrong about it.

She's older now; maybe that's why I don't like it. Not like she looks old or anything, but four years have definitely taken some of the little girl out of her face. Even though the traditional clothing is hardly the sort of thing I'd expect even Sun to wear every day, she seems to own it now. It's less like she's playing dress up.

"Smile like you normally do," I say.

"Why?"

"Because I want to take a picture of you like that."

She tries a new smile, but it looks weird.

"No, normal."

"This is normal."

"That is not normal."

She laughs, and I start clicking the shutter. The twins giggle.

"It's kinda hot under all this," she says, and lifts her skirt to ventilate her lower half. I snap a picture with her combat boots exposed.

"Now you look like some kind of action movie hero."

A grin stretches her red lips wide. "You just don't see enough *hanboks* in action movies, do you?" She takes up a fight stance. "Too bad. These things are built for movement."

The girls laugh again. "You'd fall down if you tried to fight in a dress," Liv says.

"Says you." Sun hauls her skirt up high enough to

show us the butterfly applique on the left thigh of her pants and does some kind of martial arts kick. "See? I could kick *your* ass."

"Sun!"

"Oh right. Your butt. I could kick your butt."

I frown at her.

"What?" The tassel on the side of her headdress flops into her face as she shakes her head. "Do you seriously think this is the first time they've heard the word ass? You know what that means don't you girls?"

They nod, giggling.

"See?"

"You are so not helping."

"Can I try on your hat?" Maddy asks.

"Sure." Sun beckons her closer and sets it on Maddy's baby-blond hair. The hat is too big, and the combination of Maddy's fine hair and the silk material makes it slip over her face.

"Hmm." Sun picks a bobby pin out of her hair and uses it to clamp the soft band in back so it fits Maddy's head. "There you go. Now you're a Korean princess."

Maddy folds her hands and bows to Sun, who laughs. I take picture after picture, not certain which will turn out with all the movement.

"I want to try on your dress," Liv announces.

"Sh'yeah, maybe if your sister put you on her shoulders." Sun skims a flat palm over the top of the other girl's head and bumps it into her own chest at the same height. "You wouldn't even be able to see out of the top."

"I could stand on a chair," Liv tries.

"It would look like a circus tent on you."

That's all the incentive the twins need to crawl under Sun's skirt and set up camp.

"Hey!" she protests, and I can tell by the way she's pinwheeling her arms they've made it almost impossible for her to move her feet.

"Girls!" I call, but they just giggle in reply. I'm not working too hard at stopping them, to be honest. I'm all about taking pictures.

"I am not a campground!" Sun says.

"Girls, get out of there," I try again, dropping to one knee and peeking under the blue skirt. "Come on, you two, leave Sun alone." But they just grin when I take another photograph of them instead of insisting they get out.

With a giggle, Maddy grabs the skirt from me and yanks it back down to cover them. Sun lets out a huff, and I tug the hem back up.

"Out. Now."

Whining and moaning, they emerge on all fours.

"You put it on," Liv says, pointing to me.

"Don't be bossy."

"Oh no. You're putting it on," Sun says.

"No, seriously. I just want to take the pictures. You know...." I hold up my camera. "Click, click?"

"Click-click into this getup, baby, that's how this is going down." Sun is already loosening the long red sash on her jacket. Liv takes it from her when she slips her arms free of the roomy sleeves. Beneath, the black sleeves of her t-shirt look incongruous poking out from the white straps at the top of her skirt. She reaches behind her back to untie it, then the skirt is flapping in the breeze and she shucks it into Maddy's waiting hands.

The twins bring it to me with all the reverence and skill of woodland creatures in a Disney movie and Sun indicates I should turn with a finger-twirling gesture.

"*Chima*," she intones, wrapping the bright blue skirt around my body. Long strings make a complete 360 to tie across the top of my chest. I snicker and my spine buckles when the loose ends tickle my armpits while she works. "*Jeogori*," she says next, and taps at my arms until I thread them into the billowing red sleeves. After a failed attempt to tie the sash from the front, she goes behind me again and does it that way. "I only know how to put it on myself," she mutters.

After Maddy gives up the headpiece, I'm fully outfitted.

Sun steps back to admire her handiwork. "Hmm. It's a little short on you, but other than that you look good."

"You mean apart from how I'm the color of Elmer's glue, of course."

"Oh come on, I'd at least give you..." her eyes roam in search of the right match, "oatmeal. You're definitely more oatmeal-colored."

"Great."

"I'll take your picture!" Liv shouts, hoisting my precious Canon. Instinctively I grab for it, terrified she'll drop it or smudge the lens, but she gets it under control and clicks the shutter.

"Stop moving so much," Maddy commands. "And smile."

"Say cheese!"

This goes on for a while, with the girls and Sun enjoying being on the other side of the lens for once, until eventually the twins wear down my best friend and she lets them try on her *hanbok*. Of course, they're drowning in the yards of featherweight fabric, but they love it. I'm just happy to have my camera back and I catch the whole thing in the digital memory.

After Sun's out of energy – no small feat – she and

I sit on a picnic table watching Maddy and Liv continue to attack the playground. I repack my camera in its padded bag and check my phone for messages.

"I'm thinking of calling Blake." I try to sound casual, but avoid looking at Sun.

Sun lowers her Elvis sunglasses to look at me. "Why?"

"We did go to prom together junior year. Technically I need him to recreate that picture."

"I know you're upset, but you know you should have gotten rid of anything to do with him anyway. Come on. Ex-boyfriends deserve bonfires."

I chew on the inside of my cheek for a minute, staring at the top of the picnic table. Amazing how fascinating woodgrain can be when you need it to be. Sun and I talk about everything. We've been friends since the first day of our freshman year. And we've never stopped being friends, even when I was sort-of-but-not-really dating Blake, who she was never exactly a fan of.

We were never an official couple. We just knew some of the same people, so we hung out together. You know, like friends. Friends who sometimes make out, and go to prom together, but never even go anywhere else remotely date-like. She still called him my boyfriend, which was always followed in the same breath by suggestions like "Ditch that guy" and "You can do better" and "He's such a player." When we stopped hanging out after he left for college, I figured she'd say, "I told you so," but she never said a word.

"It's not about him," I say. "I just want the picture back."

She doesn't say anything, but I'm sure she's rolling her eyes behind her big gold sunglasses.

"I won't kill me to ask him to retake the picture."

Sun straightens up as inspiration strikes her. "Maybe we can just get one of those cardboard stand-up thingies of someone actually decent and you can get your picture taken with that!"

"Like who?"

"I don't know. A storm trooper, one of those dweebs from 1Direction, who cares?"

"Just not Blake?" I interpret.

"Well..."

"Was he really that bad?"

"He makes you kind of...." She trails off then lets out a high-pitched, brainless giggle.

"Dumb?"

"Your words, not mine."

"Great."

She shifts on the table, facing me. "Why does he

make you dumb?"

I drop my face into my hands and talk through my fingers. "Because he used to call me pretty and he sounded like he meant it."

Sun pats the top of my head. "Would it help if I called you pretty?"

Laughing, I lift my face. "Maybe a little."

Her voice drips with syrup as she coos, "Who's a pretty girl? Who's so pretty? That's right! That's my pretty Mariska."

"I'm not a Labrador for God's sake!" I shove her with one foot.

She grins. "You asked."

"You volunteered!" I give her another shove for good measure.

"M'riss! I have to pee!" Olivia bellows from the far side of the playground.

I sigh. "I guess we're done."

Sun laughs into a sigh and slides off the table to stand. "I'm glad we did this."

"Me, too." I squeeze her shoulders. "Thanks."

———

LATE THAT NIGHT, when I'm uploading my pictures to

my computer, I finally realize how many I took. Nearly one hundred. Amazing how that can happen so quickly with digital. Not all of them are keepers, of course, but I have a hard time narrowing down the selection. When I get back to the first shots of Sun in her traditional poses, I look for a long time. It's not there. As much as I tried to recapture the lost moment from when we were fourteen, I didn't.

There's one picture almost identical in pose and composition to the one I remember, and yet it's so obviously not the same picture. Sun looks more like herself now, I think. Not the fourteen-year-old with the shoulder-length hair who hadn't yet learned about Manic Panic. The girl who hadn't yet stepped onto the stage with a rock band at her back. Who had never taken a scissors to a piece of clothing. Who'd never written an Op-Ed column about gender inequality in the athletics department.

As I click through all the portraits of her, though, the one I find I like the best is of her holding up her skirt enough to show off her boots and laughing. That's the girl I know. That's the picture I want to remember her by.

There are also some great ones of the LaPierre twins at their best: running across the playground with their hair streaming behind them like kite tails, or cramming their faces together and making the most awful expressions they can muster.

My favorite picture, however, is the one I took last: Maddy wearing the headpiece again, pinned in the back for size, Liv in the jeogori, her hands buried deep inside the sleeves, and Sun back in the chima, her black shirt sleeves poking out the top, her combat boots straight out in front of her as she pumps her legs on a playground swing. The girls occupy the swings to either side, Liv straddling the seat like a saddle to let her over-sized sleeves drape down, and Maddy standing on her swing, grinning face turned to her sister and Sun.

I may not have recreated my lost picture exactly, but now I have these and I never want to lose them again. I set the computer to run a back-up.

I'm never making this kind of stupid mistake again.

[7]

THE TWINS WANT to play Spa the next day. When I was little, I think we called it Beauty Shop, and it pretty much involved my friend Darla and me painting our nails and brushing each other's hair. When Olivia and Madeline LaPierre want to play Spa, they know what they're talking about. They should – their mom has taken them for enough Girls' Days at her favorite salon.

Spa is always a mixed experience for me. I get to do a lot of sitting down, being amateurishly pampered and fussed over by two eight-year-olds, but they also do my hair and make-up, and that can be a dicey outcome. They're always determined that I should keep whatever masterpiece they create with my hair, too, so when I leave the LaPierre house today, I've got small braids all around my head from the ears down.

Liv and Maddy watch me leave from the windows, making sure I can't pull out all the braids while I'm still in their sight. But as soon as my car is down the block, I start clawing out the tiny rubber bands they used to secure my stunning hairdo, but one-handed, I'm doing a better job yanking hair out than anything. I'm on my way to Caine's to pick up the yearbooks and the last thing I want to do is slow down for a hair check, so I do the best I can at stop lights. Soon, I've got a small pile of tiny purple rubber bands and broken hair in my lap.

Nothing but non-stop glamor and excitement for this girl.

I've been to Caine's house once before for a newspaper meeting, but it takes me a little squinting and slow driving to remember which one is his on the block. Then I recognize his car parked at the curb and pull in behind him. I gather all of the rubber bands in my fist and stuff them into the pocket of my capris as I head for the door. So now I've got a pocketful of tiny purple rubber bands and broken hair. Gross.

His little brother opens the door when I knock. He's a super-skinny version of Caine, with the same curly, dark hair and dark blue eyes. He even wears almost identical glasses. Can you buy glasses in bulk?

"Is Caine here?"

He doesn't answer, but backs away from the door, leaving it open for me. "Caine!" he bellows before flopping on the couch with the controller for the video game currently paused on the TV.

"Christ on a cracker, Liam, I'm right here!" Caine hollers as he comes in from the kitchen. He's got an Oreo in one hand and he startles when he sees me. "Oh."

"Did you just say Christ on a cracker?" I ask.

"Nice hair," he says.

My hands fly up to my hair and immediately find two rogue braids. How did I miss them before? I yank the rubber bands free and finger-comb them out. Caine's own fingers rake through his hair as if he's my reflection. His hair is getting to that length that officially looks shitty on guys.

WOMEN OF THE WORLD TO MEN OF THE WORLD: CUT YOUR HAIR ALREADY! See Style.

"You found my house okay?" he says before finishing his cookie.

"Yeah, it was father down the street than I remembered."

"We move it sometimes." He shrugs. "Keeps the mailman sharp."

I raise my eyebrows. "Good thinking. I usually just rearrange the numbers in the address."

"Bush league."

"So, you gonna cough up the yearbooks, or what?"

"Yeah, sure. Come on upstairs." He leads me up

the narrow stairs to a dim hallway, lit only by the sun streaming through an open door. As he passes the door, he closes it, plunging us into near-darkness.

"Whoa." I put a hand out to the wall. "What are you, a vampire?"

"Yes." A few steps down the hall, he opens another door and suddenly I can see again.

"What was that about?"

He pauses on the threshold of the second room. "My brother is a barbarian. The EPA ordered him to clean up his room but he refuses to comply."

"Seems risky."

"Apparently he'd rather go to federal prison."

"I hear they have ping pong tables."

A faint half-smile slides across his mouth. "Come on. They're in here."

I follow him into his room and stop short. It reminds me of a hotel. Or maybe a hostel is more accurate. Just a bed, dresser, desk, and chair. The only evidence anyone lives here is a laptop and a pair of small speakers on the desk – currently playing Bob Marley – and a single poster on one wall that reads: "Please Do Not Feed the Reporters." I spy a black backpack propped against the side of the desk, and the front page of the newspaper on the dresser.

"Whoa. Somebody's been packing."

"Not yet."

I make a show of looking around the room. "Where's all your stuff?"

"Right here."

"I had no idea our esteemed editor-in-chief was a monk."

"Dies irae, dies illa..."

"What?"

"Catholic joke." He shakes his head as he straightens from the desk. "Never mind."

"Seriously, Caine, where is all your stuff?"

"This is all my stuff." He pushes one side of the sliding closet doors open to reveal clothing on hangers and a single plastic crate on the floor. Kneeling, he reaches into the crate and hauls out four familiar books. Our yearbooks.

I accept the stack from his outstretched hands and sit, without thinking, on the end of his bed to open the cover of the top book. It happens to be the one from our junior year and right there on the first page is Blake's handsome face. He's not the only person on the page, but he might as well be as far as my eyes are concerned.

I turn the page so Caine won't see me blush.

Relief warms my chest at the familiar images. At least I have something now. I turn a few pages reverently and the binding crackles. It's obviously the first time anyone has opened this book. It's pristine.

"I can't believe you never even looked in here."

He shrugs and stands near my knee, head tilted awkwardly to look at the black and white display. "Didn't occur to me."

"You didn't even check if they got your senior quote right?"

"Typos give me hives. I'd rather not know."

Of course I have to check. I open the senior book on top of the junior one. He's right where he should be, Caine Fitzgibbons, looking serious. His hair was definitely shorter when the picture was taken, with some of the spiraly curls seeming to defy gravity above the others.

"'I became a journalist to come as close as possible to the heart of the world,'" I read aloud.

"Henry Luce," Caine adds. "Came out more pretentious than I wanted it to."

"At least there aren't any typos."

He bends down and pushes his glasses up to double-check. I can feel the heat of him on my shoulder and cheek, and it makes me feel itchy. "That's something anyway."

I skim over the rest of the people on the page, some friends, some barely acquaintances. They made up the scenery of the last four years of my life. Turning another page, I can almost smell the rubbery scent of hundreds of shoes on the stairs, dozens of perfumes mingling, stale smoke on some people's coats, and the hot grease of the cafeteria. I can hear the bang of locker doors and the thunder of laughter-talking-shouting-singing in the halls and the muffled sound of the piano from the music room down the hall while I sat in English last year.

Memories rush at me so fast I almost feel dizzy.

"You really don't want this?" I ask, tilting my head back to look at the side of Caine's face.

He shakes his head without looking up from the rows of smiling seniors. "Nope."

I flip through to the Activities section and find the Student Newspaper staff picture. At last, Caine can't resist the pull of the book and he lowers himself to sit beside me. Our hips press together as he leans toward the photo.

In the picture, Caine is in the center, perched on the edge of one of the work tables. He didn't want to be in the middle, I remember. We made him take the seat since he was the editor. I can see Sun's hand on one of his shoulders and I actually have my hand on his left ankle from my position on the floor. Ruthie has him by the other leg. The rest of the staff surrounds us, with Mr. O'Neill off to the side. The overall effect of the picture is one of Caine as a kidnap victim being forced to smile for the proof-of-life picture. The only thing missing was an issue of the day's paper.

"Can I ask you something?"

He straightens up a bit, but his hip and thigh are still tight to mine. "What would you do if I said no?"

I ignore that and ask, "Why were you the editor? You didn't ever want attention or anything. Why the high-profile position?"

He ticks off points on his fingers as he answers. "A. No one at our school gave a crap about who was editing the paper they didn't read. B. I want to get into journalism school, and the only position at the high school level that means anything is being the editor. C. Typos give me hives."

"What about misused apostrophes?"

He cringes. "I can't even talk about that."

I laugh. "Did an apostrophe do something horrible to you as a child?"

"Let's just say I used to have a dog."

My laughter causes the top book to fan closed and fall to the floor. I slap my hand on the bottom book to keep it from falling and find the hockey team's spread. Four pages for them, instead of the half-page group photo for the newspaper crew.

PRO-SPORTS BIAS CONTINUES UNABATED IN HIGH SCHOOLS NATIONWIDE, See Sports.

There's Blake, in his hockey gear. Behind his shield, his eyes are intense. I can even see the sweat running down his temple.

"I took that picture," I say.

Caine takes the book from my hands and holds it just inches from his face. "It's good. And considering I'm saying that about a picture of Blake Mitchell, that's really saying something."

I stiffen. "What's wrong with Blake?"

He looks at me out of the corner of his eye, then shakes his head. "Oh right. Never mind. I'm sure he's...great."

"Very sincere." I frown at him. "What's your beef with him?"

"Nothing...just, you know...it's a jock-nerd thing."

My lips feel stiff. "I guess I never thought of him as a jock."

"So you admit I'm a nerd?" Caine raises one eyebrow.

I can't help smiling. This is familiar territory. "We recognize our own."

"Never underestimate the power of a coalition of nerds with a unified purpose." He quotes the captain of our

Academic Decathlon team and I giggle, raising my fist in solidarity.

He looks like he's about to laugh with me, but instead his eyes drop from mine, toward the yearbook still spread in my lap. "It's a good picture."

I shrug, even though I know it's a good photo. "I think I only got, like, ten pictures in the yearbook in my entire four years of high school."

"Only ten, huh?" He tone tells me exactly what he thinks of that.

"I should have slept with the editor when he offered…" I say.

"Eh, I did and it didn't get me anywhere."

I smile. "Yeah, he told me."

"Jeez, you can't trust anyone." He sighs. "Show me your other pictures."

I know exactly where the ones I took are in the senior book, so I retrieve it from the floor. One of the girls' volleyball pep rally for State, one of the student council dressed like 1930s gangsters for an assembly, one of the Harry Potter Club formed in second semester, and one of Sun singing her heart out in front of her band at a school dance. I remember all of them. All taken for the paper. I could feel the edge of the stage biting into my thighs as I braced myself for the shot of Sun. Smell the sour burnt odor of the cap gun the Treasurer had gotten in trouble for firing during the assembly.

Memories, memories, memories. Dripping from every page. I close my eyes against the prick of tears that threaten me again.

"You okay?" Caine asks.

I force a smile. "I'm fine."

He pats my knee with the back of his hand, awkwardly, like he's just realized how close he's sitting. "I'm glad you're taking them."

Looking up, I see a faint reflection of myself in his glasses, superimposed over the blue of his eyes. There's a lump in my hair and a quick finger-check reveals yet another of the twins' braids.

Caine chuckles as I tug the rubber band off.

"Thanks for telling me about that." I scowl at him.

"You're welcome."

"The girls I nanny for did this. Just so you know."

"You always blame the children."

"Wouldn't you?"

"Are you saying I should get some kids just so I could blame them?"

"What other reason is there?"

He doesn't answer, but his eyes narrow as if he's studying me. Goosebumps prickle the back of my neck and

I can't hold back a nervous giggle.

"Do I have another braid somewhere?" I pat my hair with one hand.

"No." He does his hair-pushing move.

My phone starts buzzing in my back pocket and I have to lean into him to free it. It's picture mail from Sun. I recognize the photo as one she uses all the time to ask where I am. It's her, holding a map unfolded in front of her with only the top of her head and her fingers showing around the edges of the map. If I didn't already recognize it, I'd know it was old from the aqua hair. That was her color junior year, second semester. I show it to Caine. "Sun wants to know where I am."

"Why can't she text like a normal person?"

"Where's the fun in that?" I tap open my own camera and snap a quick picture of Caine's bare room and the newspaper on top of the dresser.

"What are you doing?" he asks while I type in the caption, *Guess where I am.*

"Replying."

A few seconds later, her answer comes back: *Reform school? Mental hospital?*

Laughing, I take a picture of Caine. At least the right upper quadrant of his head. The photo shows a sliver of his glasses, his dark eyebrow and a thatch of his curly hair. *Guess who I'm with.* I show the message to Caine before hitting send and he sighs.

"This is like some screwed up Where's Waldo game."

"You would make an excellent Waldo."

The phone buzzes with a final message, another old stand-by picture. Sun holding one hand up to her ear like a phone with the other hand extended to the camera, *L8R* written in black marker on her palm.

"Do you need to go so you can call her?" he asks.

Does he want me to leave? I feel my body shifting away from him on a cellular level. "I'm sure she just wants to talk about our plans for the other photos."

"How'd the one go with the – what did you call it?"

"A *hanbok*. Really good. Look." I tap into my photo file on my phone and bring up one of the pictures I took in the park.

His hand covers mine as he draws the phone closer to his face. "Oh! I honestly had no idea what you were talking about."

"Your knowledge of traditional ethnic dresses of Asia is weak, Caine." I shake my head at him sadly.

He ignores that. "It's a good picture."

"Thanks."

I nudge my backpack on the floor with one toe.

Inside, under my Canon, is a notebook now including notes on how to recreate the rest of my missing pictures. I feel squirrely with the urge to start now. I want it to be daylight, and winter, and Prom, and summer, and spring break, and my birthday, and everything at once.

"So, I don't suppose you'd be interested in helping me with any of the other pictures I'm planning? Maybe Prom?"

He shrugs, but it's not a no.

"Could be fun..." I try on a winning smile, which makes him let out a sigh/laugh combo and look away.

"Maybe."

"You're still around next week, right?" I know he's going to DePaul in Chicago, but I don't remember when they start.

"You leave before me."

"Then you *are* available..." I try the winning smile again. This time he actually smiles back, and I realize just how rarely he does it. He looks...relaxed. Happy. He should do it more often.

"I was planning on leaving home to join the circus and never coming back tonight, but you know." He shrugs.

"It can wait?" I ask.

"Eh. It kind of seems like a now or never thing."

"I guess you'll have to take up a new hobby

instead."

"I can never decide between total world domination and woodworking." He tips his face up in thought.

"Woodworking's expensive."

"There you go." Now he turns to look at me. "So, you're happy with your new picture? You're still going ahead with this, huh?"

"It's not the same, obviously, but..." I shrug. "I like it."

"You can't actually get the past back, you know that, right?"

"Yes, Professor Einstein, thank you. But I don't just want to leave it in my dust, either."

"I don't understand. It's all here, isn't it?" He taps my temple.

"Yeah, but what if I can't remember it all? What if some things are gone for good?"

"Some things are gone for good, no matter what you do to stop it."

"But it doesn't have to be like that." I squeeze the soft spot between my thumb and forefinger. "What's wrong with trying to keep a few things so you don't forget what matters?"

"Because there's no guarantee you'll be able to

keep those things. Look what happened to you."

"Okay, but how often does a person's stepfather take her stuff to the shredder?"

Caine pushes his hair back and lets out a breath I didn't know he was holding. "Stranger things have happened."

Sounds familiar. "So I should just donate all my stuff to charity and start living like a Buddhist monk like you, huh?" I want to sound breezy and teasing, but I think my tone is more like bitter and testy.

"My house burned down when I was fourteen."

Like an idiot, I gape at his clearly undamaged room.

"My old house," he clarifies. "It was an electrical fire. Started in the kitchen while we were all sleeping. Smoke detectors didn't go off. I guess my dad didn't change the batteries. Whole thing burned to the ground."

"Oh my God." Nausea wraps a fist around my guts. "Was anyone hurt?"

"My brother and my dad both got some minor burns. Everybody had smoke inhalation." He shrugs. "Liam's gerbils didn't make it."

"Oh God. I'm so sorry."

"They were just gerbils."

"That's not what I meant."

"I didn't tell you to make you feel sorry for me. I'm just saying you don't know what can happen. You can't count on things."

I want to argue with him. My throat is bubbling with a million protests, but doubt keeps them trapped. How can I possibly debate him when he's lost everything? More than I lost, that's for sure. It's like this whole time our conversation has been a giant game of rock-paper-scissors and he just came in with the ultimate weapon. Scissors cuts paper, paper covers rock...Caine's got lava. A jackhammer. Nuclear weapons, maybe.

"You really lost everything?"

He takes his glasses off and scrubs at his nose with his thumb and forefinger. "My room was directly over the kitchen. The floor collapsed." He looks down and polishes his glasses with the end of his shirt. "And whatever doesn't burn gets ruined by all the water. And the smell. You don't want anything that smells like that."

I don't know what to say. Goosebumps race along my arms and my cheeks burn with embarrassment. Over my silly tears after losing one box. Over getting Caine involved in my plans to recollect these tiny missing pieces of my life. Over the notebook in the bag at my feet.

"I'm sorry," I finally whisper.

"Don't be. It's fine." He stands and wanders a few

paces away with his hands stuffed in his pockets.

The tension around him pushes at me even at a distance. I am no longer welcome here. "Um, thanks for the yearbooks." I stand, fumbling the four large books into my arms.

"Sure. I'll walk you out." He turns to look at me, all traces of his earlier smile gone.

"That's okay. I think I remember the way."

The corner of his mouth quirks. "Don't worry, we don't move the stairs."

"Just the house."

"Right."

I nod and give him this weird mini-wave. "Bye."

All the way to the door, prickly sweat picks at the skin between my shoulders and my heart pounds. In my mind, I see my bedroom, still full of the pieces of my life, even after Ray's mistake. The silver tray on my dresser filled with junk jewelry I've collected. The framed photos on the bookshelves. Yanya, waiting for me on my bed. My pink piggy bank, my prom dress hanging in the closet, the flowers pressed in my dictionary, my boxes of books. What would I do if it were all gone?

Caine must think I am such an idiot to make a fuss over this little stuff. It's hard to believe he went along with yesterday's picture at all.

His yearbooks are heavy in my arms and my backpack takes the opportunity to slip down to one elbow. I scurry through the living room with no acknowledgement from Liam, who is back in his first-person shooter game, and let myself out the front door.

How could I take these from Caine? He's already lost everything. And even though he says he doesn't want them, I can't believe he won't regret this someday. I can't take one more thing from him. Someday, he won't be able to rely on his memory for something, and I'll be the reason he can't go back and check. I can't live with that.

I run back to the front door and leave the yearbooks in a neat pile on the porch.

[8]

BY THE TIME I get home from the LaPierres' the next day, I feel like an earthworm drying on the sidewalk after a storm. The heat and humidity were unbearable at the horse arena. The twins had their riding lessons, and my SPF 30 served the dual purpose of being inadequate protection against the sun and acting as glue for all the dust wafting up in the wake of the horses. So now I'm a dust-covered lobster.

All I want to do is shower, even though I know it's probably going to hurt on my sunburn. But I stop short when I walk into the kitchen. There is a neat stack of four yearbooks sitting on the table with a folded piece of paper on top. The paper has my name on it.

Did Ray do this? Are yearbooks the new ice cream?

It reads: *I told you not to pity me. I WANT you to have these. - C*

My arms prickle with goosebumps and I hiss at the

sting to my burn. He was supposed to keep these.

"Mom?" I call as I go deeper into the house. "Are you home?"

"Up here!"

I find her in the upstairs hall with a hammer. She's reached the re-hanging art phase of the redecoration cycle.

"Was this here when you got home?" I hold up the note.

She looks over the top of her reading glasses. "Your friend Caine stopped by earlier. He said he wanted to give you his yearbooks to replace yours?"

"Yeah...he said something about that."

"Now there's a kid after my own heart." She taps a nail into the wall and bends to select one of the frames from the row lined up at her feet. "No need to hang on to a bunch of sentimental stuff. It'll just weigh you down."

Maybe it's the fine layer of horse grit all over my hot skin. Maybe it's the stray hairs that have escaped from my hair holder and are sticking to my sweaty, pulsing, sunburned neck. Maybe it's being stonewalled by Caine. I don't know, but that's when I lose it.

"You know, just because you don't think anything that happened longer than a week ago matters doesn't make you right!"

She blinks at me in surprise, a brass nail clamped

between her lips. "Excuse me?"

"That stuff really meant something to me and I
don't need you telling me I'm too sentimental and weighed
down." Tears carve through the sweaty grit on my cheeks.

"Mariska Jean, what on earth are you talking
about?"

My chest hitches as I try to collect my breath. "I
just – I just – I just – I want my stuff back!"

"Oh Mara." My mom struggles to her feet and pulls
me into her arms. The cold, hard head of her hammer
presses into my pink skin and gives me painful
goosebumps, but it feels too good to get a hug to complain.
"Honey, I know you're upset. Of course I know how much
all that stuff meant to you." She rocks me a little, like we're
slow dancing in a crowded room.

"I'm trying so hard not to make Ray feel bad, but
it's hard! I'm..." Words spin around me, all inadequate. Sad
isn't enough. Devastated is all drama.

"Heartbroken," Mom supplies and I nod into her
shoulder. She rubs my back with her non-hammer-holding
hand. "I know you are."

"This sucks." My nose is about to drip on her so I
straighten up and sniff hard.

"You wanna know what I think?"
I nod.

"You're not gonna like it." She cups my face with one hand. "I think in a few years, this won't seem so bad."

That officially deserves a gee-thanks-for-being-so-unhelpful look.

"I told you you wouldn't like it." She shrugs. "But I'm serious. You're about to leave for college. You're about to do so much great stuff. You're going to make new friends and go places you've never been and do stuff you never even thought of doing."

The knot is back in my stomach and my heart is getting ready for a sprint.

"You'll never forget high school, I promise," she continues. "I just don't want you to think this is the end of your life."

"I know it's not."

"I'm just saying –"

"I heard you, Mom."

She frowns at me for the barest flash of a moment. "I'm only trying to help."

"I know." I look down, because I just want out of this conversation, and I don't want her to see how frustrated I am. "I'm just...I'm really hot and sweaty."

She smiles. "Why don't you go take a shower? I'm sure you'll feel a lot better after that."

I doubt it, but we've never seen eye-to-eye on

hanging onto things from the past. This road only goes around in a circle. No turn-offs. Just motion sickness.

THE IDEA FOR the signature comes to me in the shower, as ideas so often do. Sometimes I think shampoo penetrates my head and washes my brain. A clean brain is a creative brain. Maybe not.

Anyway, the point is, when I get out of the shower, I have a plan. One of those plans that requires me to act immediately. Even with a towel wrapped around my head and another one around my body.

On my way to the kitchen to get the yearbooks, I notice the rest of the pictures are still propped against the wall in the hall, but my mom and her hammer are nowhere to be found. This redecoration is going on longer than usual. I wonder if she'll even be done when I leave for Loyola.

In a week and a half.

Welcome back, knot in stomach. I missed you for those whole ten minutes you were gone. I shiver off my nerves and grab the yearbooks.

Back in my room, I find a Sharpie in my desk drawer and flip to the page where my senior picture is in the yearbook.

Hey Caine,

I'll never forget our time in the J-room. Or the
County Jail.

Cheers,

Mariska

There. Lame, but not the worst I could have come
up with. Now he'll have to keep them.

———————

I LEAVE A NOTE for my mom on kitchen counter —
she's still nowhere to be found, though if I had to guess I'd
bet she's standing in the picture hanging section of the
hardware store — and drive to Caine's house. His car isn't
there, but I knock on the door anyway. His little brother
opens it and blinks at me in the way only someone who has
been staring at a video game for too many hours can. I
wonder if you can actually become digital if you play too
long.

BOY UPLOADS BRAIN TO XBOX ONE, See
Technology.

"Caine's not here," he says.

"Yeah, I know. Can I just drop these off?"

"I guess." But he makes no move to take them from

me.

Define awkward. "So, should I just...." I lift the stack a bit. "Should I, like, put these somewhere?"

"You can leave 'em here." Liam steps back and indicates a small table near the front door.

I set the pile where he points. "Okay, well.... Thanks for all your help. You've been super."

"No problem."

Sometimes sarcasm is a total waste.

I'm halfway back to my car when the sound of a car door opening catches my attention. Caine parked across the street while I was distracted by his brother.

"What are you doing here?" he asks.

"Nice to see you, too."

"You didn't return my yearbooks, did you?"

I prop my hands on my hips as he crosses the street. "Why are you so suspicious all the time?"

"It's my CIA training. Seriously, did you bring them back?" He stops about five feet from me.

I've always found it hard to lie to someone when they ask a direct question. And he'll know the answer to this one the second he walks through the front door. Best to stall. "Why would I do that?"

"So then what are you doing here?"

"Did it occur to you I might want to say thank

you?"

"I do have a phone."

I roll my eyes. "Pardon my politeness."

He looks suspicious, but I manage to keep a straight face and he changes the subject. "So how's your project coming?"

"Good. I'm doing another shot Saturday."

"What's this one?"

"A bunch of us girls went to Virginia Beach over Spring Break. I've got a ton of pictures from the trip, but there was this one of all of us sitting on the deck at sunrise. Anna's dad took it without telling anyone. My camera was on the kitchen counter at the beach house, so...." I shrug.

"So you're flying to Virginia Saturday?"

I nod. "Yes, in my private jet."

"How are you going to do it, really?"

"I'm willing to live without the ocean. It's the sunrise I really want."

"Why?"

I blink. "What do you mean why?"

"Why the sunrise?"

My memory shifts back to that morning. We'd stayed up all night, the five of us. Probably we kept Anna's parents awake too, but I don't remember. It was cool and damp on the beach in the predawn light, and we were all quiet. We were exhausted, but as long as we'd stayed up this long, we figured we should see the sunrise. I remember sitting between Sun and Cori, the three of us huddled and shivering under a big striped beach towel.

"Because it was beautiful," I say. "And because I remember how it felt to be sitting there with my friends. It was...nice."

"You can do better than that."

I frown at him. "Because it was just this quiet, comfortable moment when we were all just...there. Alone. But together. Do you know what I mean?"

The corner of his mouth lifts. "That's better."

"Why do you even care?"

"I'm just trying to understand this quest of yours."

"I'd hardly call it a quest."

"Well, whatever it is, I want to understand it."

"What is so hard to understand? I lost some pictures that were really important to me and I'm trying to get them back." I try to cross my arms, but my sunburn feels tight and itchy across my back like that.

"But do you seriously not remember these things without the pictures? What you just told me proves you do remember."

"That's not the point."

"That's exactly the point."

"God, you're impossible." I am striking out all over on the conversation front today. The burnt parts of my skin are hot and stiff, the unburnt parts are suddenly chilled and prickly. "I want them, okay? I want to look back in ten years and remember what it was like to be there."

"And you can't do that without the pictures."

I try again to cross my arms, but the burn stops me. It's making me restless to be so restricted. "I'd prefer not to, okay? Why does it have to be some major character flaw to want something?"

"It's not. But you can't always just go back and redo things."

"I'm getting close."

He opens his mouth, but nothing comes out. He does the hair-shoving thing and sighs. "Okay, good. I'm glad it's working out."

"Very sincere, Caine."

"This really isn't any of my business." He lets his hair fall back into place and stuffs his hands in his pockets. "I shouldn't be bugging you about it."

It's such a sudden shift in gears I can't make my brain work. "Yeah. Okay. No problem."

"So, you were leaving?" he asks, stepping out of my path.

"I was."

"Okay. Catch you later." He nods once, and then he's past me and heading for the front door.

I remember the yearbooks just inside and make a break for my car. I need to make a clean getaway. I've got the ignition on and the car in gear when Caine throws open the front door.

I wave through the window and gun it.

———

MY THUMB HOVERS over the message icon beside Blake's name while I pace. I feel like Hamlet. To text or not to text, that is the question. In my mind, images flip back and forth — Blake and me in front of the backdrop of stars at prom, then Sun's barely concealed disapproval sitting on the picnic bench yesterday. He *is* a sort-of ex-boyfriend, and he *did* do a total disappearing act after he left for school. Maybe I'm an idiot for thinking he'll help me.

Then again, it wasn't really even a breakup. It wasn't like he hated me. This should be no big deal, right?

This is pathetic.

I tap into a message and quickly type, *Hey Blake, any chance you're in town right now? I have a strange favor to ask you.*

And then I wait. And pace.

Eventually I get a reply. *Who is this?*

Which is when my heart takes an express elevator to my feet. He doesn't even remember me. How humiliating.

Now that my dignity has been crushed, I have nothing to lose, so I reply, *Mariska Bokori. From high school.*

This time the answer is almost instant. *Hey pretty girl. Long time no see.*

Okay so maybe he just didn't have my name associated with the number. We start a fast flurry of messages.

Me: *Are you home for the summer?*

Him: *Yes. Move in to my new place next week.*

Me: *I'm doing kind of a photo project and I was hoping you'd be able to help.*

Him: *I'm up at Wadi's cabin right now. I'll text you when I get back.*

Me: *Great! Thanks!*

As soon as I hit send, I regret the exclamation points. I feel like my roommate Briony.

No, she would have used emojis.

The thought makes me laugh out loud. There's no good reason, other than a sense of accomplishment that's whirling through me. Sending that text feels as good as slaying a dragon now that it's over.

Well, maybe that's an exaggeration. Whatever.

Right now, even though I was planning to head for bed, I'm on high alert. I feel like I could climb a mountain. Well, maybe I could speed read some Tolstoy or something less physically challenging than mountain climbing.

In reality, I should be unpacking the bags of stuff my mom's been bringing home from Target, putting all the toothpaste, bandages, Tylenol, and stuff into the plastic box she got for me to take to my dorm room. But I think my time could be better spent re-reading *Harry Potter and the Deathly Hallows* with my decrepit teddy bear Yanya under my arm.

Good, rational decision-making. That's what that is.

I won't think about Blake.

I won't think about my lost stuff.

I won't think about college.

———

IN THE MORNING, I find Caine's yearbooks piled on the hood of my car. I skim through the senior edition, but there's no sign he retaliated for my message. I can't even tell if he saw it.

This will not stand.

———

After work, I cruise by his house again and, finding no sign of his car, decide to leave the books on the front steps again.

To the inside of the front cover, I have added Property of Caine Fitzgibbon in large, silver letters right over the exterior shot of the school. I do love my Sharpie collection.

After I drop the stack on the porch, I dig a piece of paper out of my backpack – a napkin from the coffee shop, actually – and use it to mark the page where I wrote the first note.

There. Now he'll understand what a yearbook is for and stop being so pigheaded.

POT CALLS KETTLE BLACK, See Politics & World News.

[9]

EVEN THOUGH IT'S still dark when my alarm clock goes off Saturday morning, I'm fully awake in less than a second. I sit up in bed, accidentally pulling the covers off of Sun, who slept over in preparation for our pre-dawn excursion. She groans and gropes for the blankets, determined to pull them over her head, but I won't let her. Instead, she curls into a fetal position and peeks at me through one eye.

"Just so you know, I hate you."

"That's okay," I say. "As long as you get up."

"What was I thinking when I agreed to this?"

"How incredibly awesome your best friend is? How much you want to help her in her hour of need?"

"Yeah, that must have been it." She rolls onto her knees and buries her head under her arms.

I leave her that way and slip my favorite pajama pants over the cotton boxers I slept in. Then I pull on the hooded sweatshirt I've co-opted from Ray and rake my fingers through my hair.

By now, Sun has planted her hands on my bed and stretched her butt up toward the ceiling in some bizarre Sun version of yoga. She stretches herself slowly to a standing position and glares at me. "Happy?"

"Very."

She steps off the bed and shrugs into a flannel shirt. Adding cut-off sweatpants to her ensemble, she checks herself in the mirror. "Oh good God."

"You look great," I say. "Come on."

"You owe me," she mutters, but shoves her feet into her soft fleece boots and heads for the door.

———

THE SKY IS lightening as we drive to Cori's house, but it's still a deep blue. It looks like it's been painted on some invisible ceiling – lower than the usual sky – like I could gather handfuls of it, stain my hands indigo, if only I stood on top of a tall building.

We keep the music low, just something to keep the night at arm's length, and don't talk much. Sun's got her feet pulled up on the seat with her arms wrapped around her knees. Even in August, you can't help but get the chills at this hour of the day. I kill the headlights when I come to idle in front of Cori's, and dial her number. I dare not honk the horn for fear of waking her younger siblings. Her mom would have all our heads.

She doesn't answer, but I see the light come on in her window. In a couple of quiet minutes, Cori and Anna shuffle onto the porch. Anna lifts a hand to us before wrapping her arms around her body. They're in pajamas, just like us. I smile.

It's amazing what true friends will do for you. And you just know it, too. They might put on a show of fussing about it, or tell you how much you owe them, but they'll do it, whatever it is. I am going to miss the safety of this kind of friendship when we all have to go our separate ways. I know we'll always have each other, and I know there will be new friends in college, but our friendship, the way it is now, it's life expectancy is running out.

Anna crawls into the backseat and Cori climbs in, nearly on top of her, so they look like a couple of sleeping puppies.

"It's so early," Cori yawns.

"Why are we doing this again?" Anna wants to know.

"Something about how we love M'riss and want to help her," Sun mumbles.

"Oh, right."

"I don't have to get up at the ass crack of dawn for any of your other schemes after this, do I?" Cori asks.

"Nope. No more dawn. Promise."

"Good," Anna says.

"You guys are coming to Second Prom, right?" Sun props her cheek on the back of the passenger seat, trying to look at the girls behind her.

They both mumble some kind of assent. I smile to myself in the semi-dark, and blink furiously so I can focus on the road.

"Stupid Monica and her stupid summer camp," Cori mutters. Monica, the fifth member of our spring break trip, is off counseling impressionable youth at some kind of camp for brilliant musicians, so she can't be a part of my re-creation.

"Where are we doing this?" Anna asks.

"Well…." I glance in the rearview mirror. "It's not going to be perfect…"

Sun snorts.

"What?" Cori's tone is flat.

"Just trust me."

But they're awake now. Curiosity has that effect on people. They want details. And the more they beg, the less I want to tell. I've got excited butterflies in my stomach, being the one who knows where we're going. There is something so delicious about holding in a surprise.

They pester me, and I turn up the radio. The sky looks less like velvet now. Light seems to come from the air itself. I give the car a little more gas to beat the sunrise.

Cori and Anna are alternating suggestions as we drive now:

"The pool at the Riv!"

"The water hazard at the golf course!"

"The waste treatment plant!"

"A really big puddle!"

At last, I park on the street near one of the trail markers for the cross-county bike path.

"I'm not riding anywhere on a bike at this hour of the morning," Cori declares.

"We don't have any bikes, dummy," Sun says.

"Just come on, you guys."

Out of the car, I shiver in the chill. My sunburn is faded, except in a few prime places where heat still radiates from my skin, but it still hurts to shower. And get goosebumps, as it turns out. The other girls are hunched, too, rubbing their arms for warmth.

"After you, Fearless Leader," Sun says.

I settle my backpack carefully onto my shoulders – ow – and cross the bike path at a diagonal to meet the footpath on the other side. I can't resist checking up and down the empty, sleeping street, but there isn't a cop in sight. We're on county park territory now, and technically, the park is closed. I've been shooed out of a park at closing time, that's for sure, but I've never been here at the opposite end of the time spectrum.

"Are we supposed to be here?" Anna puts words to my thoughts.

"Technically?" I ask without answering.

"You have to understand," Sun supplies, "Mariska here is a woman on a quest. Laws do not apply."

We all giggle at that as we disappear into the tree line. The sound of the nearby river is clear now, and in a moment we make gentle trip-trapping sounds as we cross the footbridge.

"Don't tell me this...stream is going to stand in for the ocean," Cori says.

"Seriously, Cori, could you be more negative this morning?"

"I can't be held responsible for my actions before the sun is up."

Sun growls at her in a pirate voice, "Into the drink with ye, ye scurvy dog!" She hooks Cori's arm over her shoulder and hunches her back like she's trying to get the leverage to launch her off the bridge.

"Hey!" Cori protests.

"Walk the plank!" Anna chimes in, scrabbling after Cori's feet, and knocking one of her slippers to the ground.

"Ack! My foot!" Cori howls. "The pajama pirates have my slipper!"

Anna and Sun let out a simultaneous "Arrrrr!" before dissolving into laughter.

I manage to get my camera loose quickly enough to get pictures of them once Cori is nearly upside down with the toes of her one bare foot splayed out like a chimp. Anna's got her around the hips, but Cori's got a handful of Anna's fleece coffee-cup-patterned robe and she's not letting go. Sun is hunkered down below Cori. Their elbows are linked in some crazy way I can't figure out at first glance, and their heads are only a tangle of Sun's wild red color hair and Cori's red curls. All of it is muted by the filter of pre-dawn light.

Suddenly, Sun loses her balance and the three of them go down in a heap of legs, arms, bedhead, and pajamas. Assorted groans rise from the pile.

"I think there's gravel in my mouth." Sun's voice is muffled.

"You guys should consider trying out for the Olympics," I tell them, circling them to get pictures from fresh angles.

"People who get other people out of bed before

sunrise should not mock those they got out of bed." Cori spits out a rogue curl.

"Yeah, no kidding!" Anna pushes herself off the heap and cranes her neck to look at me. "You gonna help us up or what?"

I hook my camera around my neck and offer my hands to Anna. After a little effort, we get everyone back on their feet. Sun does, in fact, have gravel stuck to her lips.

"You guys are, like, the worst pirates ever," I say.

"That's it!" Cori slaps her hands on her thighs. "You better hang onto that camera, M'riss..."

Thank God I put on my awesome Ugg slippers with the backs this morning, because I easily stay ahead of Cori in her fluffy terrycloth flip-flops. Sun and Anna are more of a threat, but neither of them really seems to want to catch me. They just follow as I run along the dirt trail, deeper into the park, hoping nothing jumps out of the shadowed trees. I keep the river to my left as we head slightly south. When we're nearly there, Sun figures it out and outpaces me. The *woof, woof* of her boots make her sound like she's running through acres of stuffed animals.

And then, just as the sky above the tree line blossoms into the powdery pink of dawn, we reach the skating pond. It's not frozen now, of course. Instead it's filled with lily pads, cattails, and the *chir-rup!* of crickets and *ree-deep* of frogs signing off for the night. They'll pass the watch of the pond to the cicadas and dragonflies in a few minutes.

We have to hurry.

"There." I point to the flagstone patio jutting out from the warming building to the west. In the winter, the firebowl in the center crackles constantly while skaters and their audience try to stay warm. In the summer, it's nothing but a still life. But the wooden railing is just like I remembered, and just enough like the railing at the beach house to make it worth trespassing.

"Nice pick, Mariska," Sun says before bending forward with her hands on her knees to catch her breath.

Anna and Cori catch up to us, both panting. Even though my lungs are screaming with the effort of our run, I know I've got to keep moving. I climb the uneven steps to the patio and unload my backpack. I've got my flexible mini-tripod and a random collection of stuff I've used before to prop it just right.

"Can you guys get in place?" I point to the railing and my friends drop gratefully to the ground, their legs hanging off the edge of the patio. There's enough room between upright supports on the railing for all four of us to fit. Anna props her chin on the long crossbar while I lie across the edge of the firepit to check the viewfinder of my camera.

A pack of cards under one tripod leg, three packets of sugar under another and I'm ready. I double-check the settings are the way I want just as the first sliver of sun pokes over the top of the trees to the east. I scoop up the remote control and run across the patio to dive into the space left by Cori and Sun. Sun wraps an arm around my waist and rests her head on my shoulder.

"Thank you so much, you guys," I say, squeezing Cori's hand.

"You're welcome," Anna says, turning to smile at me.

I click the remote control in my hand several times while the sun rises higher in the sky. The birds are calling excitedly in the trees all around us.

"All right, I admit it – this isn't the worst thing I've ever done," Cori says after a while.

"Yeah, it's kind of nice," Anna agrees.

"As long as my slippers don't fall into that nasty pond, I'll be happy." Cori sticks her legs straight out to reveal her toes scrunched tight around the thong of her fuzzy flip flops.

We all poke our heads through the railing to look down at the murky water of the pond. It's no great thing of beauty, that's for sure. Unless maybe you're a frog.

"Remember when Monica fell off the pier?" Anna laughs.

"Something touched me! Something touched my leg!" Cori shrieks in imitation.

"I'm gonna die!" Sun wails.

"My shoe fell off!" I claw at Sun and Cori. "A shark took my shoe!"

We're all laughing, remembering our poor friend flailing in water only four feet deep. She didn't realize it, of course, with all the thrashing and screaming. We all ended up in the ocean that night, though only Monica went in with her shoes.

"It sucks she's not here," Anna says, wiping laughter from her eyes.

"She'll be so bummed she missed this." Cori puts me and Anna into a headlock/hug.

"Excuse me!" A voice startles us all into awareness. I look around for the source with a pounding heart. To my right, where the footpath disappears into a curve around the south end of the skating pond, a cop on a bicycle has just come into view.

"Oh crap," Sun mutters.

Anna's already on her feet. "Good morning, Officer!"

"Are you girls aware the park is closed?"

"Is it?" Anna asks. Cori, Sun, and I stand up, and I back slowly toward my backpack and camera.

"Miss, stop moving please."

I freeze, and the cop sets the kickstand on his bike as Sun stifles a laugh.

"*Shut up*," Cori hisses.

As the cop climbs the stairs, I have an almost irresistible urge to put my hands in the air like I'm being robbed. The others are staring at me, Sun with her hands clapped over her mouth.

"All right, I'm gonna need to see ID from all of you," he says when he's on the same level as us. "And you – " he points to me. "I'm gonna need to take a look in your bag, is that a problem for you?"

"No." I shake my head. My hands are levitating about six inches away from my body. I can't decide what to do with them. He doesn't move toward the bag, so I just stand there like a half-assed airplane with my eyes so wide I can feel the wind in them.

"I'm gonna need you to open it for me."

"You don't have to do it!" Sun blurts out. "He can't look without your permission."

"Sun, shut up!" Anna says through clenched teeth.

"Do you have a problem opening your bag for

me?" the cop asks me.

I shake my head. "I don't think so."

"Then why don't you go ahead and open it."

With my arms still out like a ballerina, I close the distance to my backpack and heft it, peeling back the front flap to show him.

He looks inside, then up at me. "That's, uh...quite a collection of things you have there. Just what are you girls up to?"

"Taking a picture." I jut my elbow to the camera, still propped on its assemblage of junk.

The cop – Officer Davies, according to his nameplate – raises one eyebrow.

The story spills out of me like a flood. I'm talking too fast and sweating.

"You are aware the park is still closed at this hour?" he asks.

"I guess so."

He asks me for an ID, and luckily I dropped my wallet into my backpack before I left the house. I show him my driver's license.

"Mariska?" he asks. I nod. "If I call in your license number what am I going to find out about you?" He props one hand on the radio clipped to his shoulder.

"Nothing." I shake my head frantically.

"Nothing?"

"Really. Nothing. I'm a good kid."

"She's super boring," Anna adds, and I don't even have the guts to give her a look.

"Kind of ironic, don't you think?" Officer Davies hands me back my license.

"Why?"

"Considering you've got the word 'risk' right in the middle of your name?"

I blink in shock. Is he joking? Is this cop seriously teasing me instead of arresting me? "What are you saying?" I ask.

He props his hands on his gun belt. "Go home. All of you. Stop trespassing."

"Thank you," I whisper, and whip around to start stuffing everything in my backpack.

"Hey, can we get a picture with you?" Cori asks.

Whirling to face her, I give her bug eyes. Why is everyone messing with me this morning?

To my amazement, Officer Davies seems to be smiling. "Are you joking?"

"Is that illegal?" Cori says.

He hooks his thumbs into his belt, squinting at us with an unreadable expression. We're so going to get arrested. Tickets, at the very least. We were free to go and now Cori is going to get me arrested because she's an idiot. Why did my first encounter with the police have to be after I was eighteen? I'm going to be charged as an adult!

Then just as I'm getting ready to hyperventilate, Office Davies shrugs and says, "Why the hell not?"

"Sweet!" Anna claps her hands. She flaps a hand at me to set the camera back on its tripod, which I just barely manage with shaking hands.

"Can I hold your gun?" Sun asks.

"No." No joking tone this time.

"I had to ask." She grins at him.

"Come on, Risky, let's go!" Cori says, waving me into the picture.

"Risky?" I repeat.

She laughs. "We don't need perfection."

"Okay, okay...." I rush into the shot, where Anna throws her arms around my waist. Using the remote, I snap three shots.

"Thank you!" Sun says to the officer. "You rule!"

"Just do me a favor and get out of the park, okay?"

"We're going."

With my backpack secured on my sore shoulders, we hightail it down the footpath back in the direction we came. No one feels safe laughing until we're on the other side of the wooden bridge, but then it's all we can do to say upright.

"You almost got us arrested!" Cori howls. "I can't believe I almost got arrested in my pajamas at a stinky pond."

"That was ridiculous," I say. "I can't believe he let us go!"

"You still think Monica will be jealous?" Anna giggles.

"Abso-fucking-lutely," Sun says.

"I owe you guys so big," I say.

"You can start with breakfast," Cori says. "I'm starving."

"Ooh, bacon..." Sun moans.

"Are we going in our pajamas?" Anna grins.

I grin. "Definitely."

[10]

THE YEARBOOKS ARE stacked on my front porch when I get home.

"Damn it, Caine!" I mumble as I throw the car into park.

"What are you talking about?" Sun asks.

"He brought them back again." I get out of the car, and stalk to the front of the house. There's a Post-It note on top this time.

Keep them. – C

"What's going on with this?" Sun peeps over my shoulder.

I explain the yearbook battle, but the words don't really seem to do it justice. Sun looks confused, that's for sure. "Never mind." I tuck the books under my arm. "I'll take care of it."

"There's something inside." Sun tugs at a little slip

of paper poking out of the senior edition, but it won't budge. Another Post-It, I guess.

Cupping my hand over the little flap of paper, I feel my insides squirm. "Probably just some smart ass remark. You know Caine."

Sun cocks an eyebrow, but doesn't say anything.

"You know what makes me really happy?" I ask. "Not having to tell my parents I've been arrested for trespassing right now."

She laughs, and allows the change of subject. Excellent quality in a best friend.

I wait until she's safely in the shower before I open the marked page in Caine's yearbook. I don't know why exactly I don't want her to see whatever is in there, but I know I don't. He's marked the page where his own picture is, and used a red marker to write a note that covers about a quarter of the page.

Mariska,

What could I say about you that hasn't already been said by the FBI? I'll never forget all that you did for me that night in Berlin. And don't worry, when I promise to keep a secret, I take that secret to my grave. Just swear to me you'll be more careful who you photograph from now on. I've only got so many favors in so many government

offices and god knows I need to keep one for myself.
    - C

My need to retaliate and outdo him is immediate and complete. My fingers are already curling around an imaginary Sharpie as I start planning my reply. This cannot stand.

I flip to the newspaper staff photo and start writing immediately. I don't even have to think about.

Mr. Fitzgibbon,

Since you appear resistant to the usual methods of persuasion we present the following logical argument.

Dentist = Pain and Suffering, therefore

Waiting Room at Dentist = Waiting for Pain and Suffering, and

College = No Pain and Suffering (theoretically), therefore

High School does not = Waiting Room at Dentist, therefore

Yearbook > Highlights Magazine.

We now consider this matter closed.
Regards,

Mariska Bokori
President of the Committee to Save Caine
Fitzgibbon From Himself

I don't know what it is about Caine that inspires me to these bizarre flights of fancy, but they come as easily as breathing when I'm around him. Or, apparently, writing to him.

Before I can think too much about what I've done, I slam the book shut. I'm putting it at the bottom of the pile just as Sun returns from the bathroom.

"So, what's next on the list?" she asks.

"Numerically? Clown soccer."

She recoils. "We're not actually doing that one, are we?"

And even though a second ago, I felt overwhelmed at the idea, her protest stings. "Don't act so shocked. It was on the list."

"Yeah, but I didn't think you were serious about that one."

"Why not?"

"Where the hell are we going to find another group of clowns playing pick-up soccer?"

"Um...I'm working on that." Truth is, I have no clue. Not a single clue.

Sun walks heel-toe-heel-toe like a tightrope walker toward me, her eyes down to watch her progress. "M'riss, I think we need to accept that this one is gone for good."

I flop back on the bed. "They're all gone for good, Sun."

"Well, then what's the point of all this?" She perches on the edge of the mattress with her arms wrapped around her body to keep her towel up.

"I don't know," I sigh, cupping my hands over my face.

"I thought you were happy with the pictures we've been getting."

"I am." I uncover my face for a moment to look at her. "I think I am." My eyes sting enough for me to pinch the bridge of my nose.

Sun rubs my knee. "You're not happy."

"No – " That sounded watery and pathetic. I look up toward my eyebrows and force a breath. "No, it's not that. I'm happy. I think. But I'm not stupid – they're not the same pictures."

"Duh."

"Maybe I should just call it off. What's the point of all this?"

"If you want." She shrugs.

Instantly, my nerves jump like I've been shocked

and my heart kick starts into high gear. "No."

"I figured." This time she grins.

"I just wish I could get my old pictures back and I wouldn't have to worry about this." I can see one of the bigger holes left in my wall from this angle, and I can't resist rubbing my fingertip across it. Soon it will be spackled, primed, and buried under a fresh coat of paint. Good bye, hole. Good bye, pretty pale blue walls.

Sun interrupts my thoughts. "Well, since that's not an option, I'd advise you get over it."

"Very helpful, thank you." I decide to go back to hiding my eyes under my arm.

"I'm just saying – what is it my grandpa says? – wish in one hand, shit in the other, and see which one fills up first."

Okay, no matter how much I want to wallow, that makes my mouth twitch. "Point taken."

"Besides, I don't know about you, but I've had fun so far."

It's a fair point. I wouldn't have climbed back into O'Neill's car, gotten such great pictures of the twins, or had breakfast with my closest friends in our pajamas if we hadn't started all this. But, in a way, that's just the problem. I'm trying to get back what I lost, and instead I keep making these new memories that don't have anything to do with the old ones.

And now, the biggest problem of all looms ahead.

I groan. "What was I thinking? How can I ever hope to do anything remotely as good as Clown Soccer?"

She giggles, but tries to stuff it back inside and ends up snorting.

"What's so funny?"

"I just can't believe we're having a conversation that includes the phrase clown soccer." She lets out one last helpless giggle. "God, that was the best day."

JAZZ IN THE PARK was always a sampler platter of summer goodness: sultry air, with just the right amount of breeze; good friends sprawled out on blankets; and the acrid tang of bug spray licked off your fingers as you try to eat the snacks you brought. When you live in a cold climate, summer vibrates with energy and enthusiasm, and we were determined to soak up as much of it as possible in the weeks before starting our senior year of high school.

Sun's friend Myra drove, because she had access to her parents' minivan, and the rest of us kept our faces pressed to the windows as she circled block after block looking for street parking. It was never easy to find a spot downtown, but on Jazz in the Park nights, you might as well look for a unicorn.

"There!" Chris shouted, jabbing his finger into the window in his haste.

Myra broke several laws turning the van around and backing down a one-way street to the spot thirty yards from the corner. Equal congratulations went to Chris for his eagle eyes, and Myra for her Hollywood stunt driver-like skills as we unloaded from the van with our arms full of Jazz in the Park enjoyment necessities.

"All right, everyone memorize where we're parked or we're screwed later," Myra said.

Everyone looked around and shouted out landmarks as we started for the corner.

"We're right by the MSOE athletic field," someone said as we crossed the street.

Chris was the first to notice. "Are those...clowns?"

All conversation ceased as we shaded our eyes to peer up at the field on top of the parking structure. It did look like a couple of clowns were leaning on the fence.

We looked at each other and without having to talk about it, found our way to the nearest entrance. We rushed up the stairs to the roof for a closer look.

Yes, there were clowns running around on the athletic field. They appeared to be...playing soccer.

"Am I really seeing this?" Sun asked.

"I think you are."

"What the hell?"

Which about summed it up. Twenty-odd people in full clown make-up, wearing wigs, and hats, and clown costumes of every description, were sprinting back and forth on the scrubby field with a metallic orange soccer ball.

"I hate clowns," Myra said softly, but her tone was one of wonder, not disgust.

"What do you suppose they're doing?" I asked.

"Playing soccer," someone – Chris, I think – answered.

"But...why?"

"Let's go ask." Sun. Of course.

We found the entrance to the field and walked to the sidelines of the game, where a few more clowns were waiting to sub in, cheering for their teammates or sipping on water bottles. When Sun asked what was going on, the only answer we got was, "Just a pick-up game."

Whether they were determined to be mysterious, or genuinely didn't grasp the deep surreality of the moment, the clowns never offered us an explanation. Nor, I think now, did we really want one.

Of course I had my camera, and although the

lighting was terrible, I took a few shots. None of them did the spectacle justice. It's like how you can see the Grand Canyon a million times on the Discovery Channel, but until you've stood on the lookout point in person, your jaw doesn't drop.

We spent the rest of the evening in a state of happy shock. Nothing, it seemed, could distract us from the strangeness of what had happened. Conversation turned to Clown Soccer over and over again. More than one person suggested we'd shared some kind of group hallucination. Perhaps we'd walked through a cloud of some powerful drug, or fumes when we'd gotten out of the van.

Part of me expected the clowns to still be there when we went back to the parking spot, hours later. Of course they were gone.

It remains the oddest experience of my life to this day.

"SO, OKAY, WE can't actually recreate the weirdness that is Clown Soccer, right?" Sun says.

"Right." I sigh.

"Would it help if we just found some clowns, like at the circus or something, and handed them a soccer ball?"

A burst of laughter jumps out of me. "Oh, hey clowns, nice circus. Would you hold this for me while I get a picture?" I mimic passing a soccer ball to an unseen clown.

Sun grins. "It could work."

"A, I don't know where we'd find these clowns. B, I think that would be a little too weird, even for clowns."

"So we're not doing that one?" she asks.

I shake my head. "I don't know. I wish there was some way."

Neither of us speaks for a minute, lost in thought.

My phone rings, a welcome distraction, and my pulse rushes back to warp speed when I see Blake's name on the readout. I curl to a sitting position, eyes wide and palms instantly sweaty. "Hello?"

"Hey, Pretty Girl."

I mouth "It's Blake," to Sun, who fakes surprise, rolls her eyes, then gets off the bed to replace her towel with some actual clothing.

"How's your trip?" I ask Blake, giving in to my urge to pace. The room is still a disaster, and with Sun moving around, I have even less room than before. I'm pretty much turning in circles.

"Oh it's been great." Blake launches into a story about the JetSki, and something about fishing, I think. I have to confess to having about as much interest in the great outdoors as I do in helping my mother pick out a new paint color for my room. Plus, I'm completely self-conscious that he caught me in my pajamas with my hair in a failing ponytail. He can sense it, I'm sure. "...anyway, we came back to the nearest town so I thought I'd give you a call, see how you were doin'."

I smile. "I'm doing fine!"

Across the room, Sun pauses with her shirt gathered in her hands, to give me a look. It says, Yeah, whatever, you big liar.

I ignore her. "Just redid another picture this morning."

He laughs. "You're still working on that?"

It's only been two, I think, but answer, "Yeah. It's going pretty well." I slip a fingernail between my teeth, but don't let myself bite. He doesn't need to hear that. All I want to do is ask him if he'll come to the prom recreation, but I don't think we're in that kind of place yet.

"Glad you're having fun, Pretty Girl. Listen, the guys are flagging me down. I gotta run. Talk to you soon, though, right?"

"Right!"

He disconnects kind of abruptly. I imagine the guys starting the car and threatening to leave without him.

It would be typical of Blake's crowd of guys.

When I put my phone down and come back to the reality of my bedroom, Sun is back on my bed, perched on the end in her usual way. She's dressed now, and inspecting her nail polish.

"Sorry about that," I say.

"No biggie. It was actually kind of fun." She looks up with a glint in her eye. "He makes you talk in an octave only dogs can hear."

"Wha--uh!" I cross my arms. "That's not true!"

"It so is." Holding an imaginary phone up to her ear, she uses a squeak only a mouse could love, imitating me. "Just redid another picture this morning!"

Snatching up a pillow, I launch it at her. "Shut up!"

She laughs and bats it back at me. "I'm not saying it's bad. You can't help yourself."

"I can, too!" I give her another wallop with the pillow. "You're mean."

"Hey, everyone's allowed to be a little stupid when they're around a crush." She holds up to placating hands. "As long as it doesn't go on forever."

"It's not like we're not dating. It's just...a thing."

"A thing." She thinks about that. "I've seen you around other guys at this stage, and I promise you, this is worse than usual."

"He makes me...pleasantly nervous."

She rolls her eyes. "Sounds like you need some Tums."

"Oh come on, don't you like that feeling? What about before you go on stage for a show?"

"I always feel like I have to pee."

"Gross."

She laughs. "I know the feeling you're talking about it. But, honestly? No. I like the part where I'm already on stage and the jitters are gone. I like killing it and the crowd is so into it and it's just fucking awesome." She closes her eyes and shivers. "That's the good part. The trusting myself part. The part where everyone is in sync and it's just...awesome."

She makes the next stage sound good. It sounds a lot like the thrumming feeling of happiness and safety with Sun, Cori, and Anna at the pond this morning. My nail is back between my teeth and I give in to the urge to bite it.

"I want to do Clown Soccer," I blurt.

Sun's smile could light a church full of candles. "Good. I want to, too."

"I just have no idea how."

"What we need is a time machine. Then we could go back in time and get another picture of them. Digital this time."

"If I had a time machine, I'd just go back and stop Ray from taking the box in the first place." I laugh.

"Oh. Right. That would be easier." Sun sighs. "But I think I would seriously go back and see Clown Soccer again. It was just so weird."

"Maybe that's what we should do." I stand up, the idea propelling me to my feet. "Not Clown Soccer, but just something really weird."

She raises her eyebrows. "Like what?"

"I don't know yet. But what if we did something that would be just as strange and mysterious and wonderful for other people as Clown Soccer was for us?"

Now a smile lifts the corner of her mouth. "I like it. We could totally do that."

Pressing my palms together, I rest my fingers against my mouth. "The only question is, what?"

[11]

Caine's mom answers the door when I stop by with
the yearbooks. She looks like him, with the same
corkscrews of dark brown hair, though hers graze her
shoulders and have obviously met with product and styling
– foreign concepts to her son.

"Mariska, right?" she says.

My eyes widen. "Yeah. Good memory."

"Caine said you might be stopping by." She smiles.
"He's not up yet, sorry. I can wake him if you want."

"No, that's great. It's better this way."

She looks confused, so I continue. "He keeps
trying to give me these, and I want him to keep them." I pat
the stack of books with one hand.

"Who do they *actually* belong to?" she asks.

"They're his." That feels too mysterious. "I lost
mine. He said I could have his, but..." I shrug. I think I'm
talking too much.

She tilts her head to the side with an exasperated

look. "He's trying to give away his yearbooks?"

"I won't let him!" I assure her, shifting the books to hold them out to her.

"Good." She takes the books from me, then hesitates. "Would you like to come in and wait for him?"

"Um..." In truth, I want to flee the scene before he discovers I was here, but I'm not sure how to say no.

"Ah, you want a clean getaway," she says.

"Well, us master criminal types don't usually hang around, right?"

She smiles again. "I see why he likes you."

My stomach contracts unexpectedly. "I...uh..."

Her smile widens. "If you'd like, I can hide these in his room so he doesn't know they're back."

"What would you hide them behind?" The words are out before I know I'm going to say them. "There's nothing in there."

Her laughter is a feminine version of the throaty chuckle I heard from Caine now and again. "I keep telling him Witness Relocation isn't going to move us again any time soon, but he just won't settle in."

It takes me a beat to realize she's joking. "I think he's more afraid of his bookie." It must be something about Fitzgibbons DNA that makes my brain go all weird like this.

She laughs again, and I find myself joining in. Then a sudden sound from the depths of the house cuts us short.

"*It's okay!*" a disembodied voice calls.

Mrs. Fitzgibbons rolls her eyes. "Well, thank you, Mariska, for making my son act like a normal teenager. I'll make sure he gets these. And keeps them."

"Thanks." I give a little wave as she closes the door.

[12]

I CAN'T HELP expecting Blake to text that afternoon. He was gone last time we messaged each other and that was a few days ago – it seems likely he'll be home on Sunday. I know it's ridiculous, but I keep checking the volume on my ringer and thumbing my way into the call log just in case I missed something.

IMPATIENCE AND WISHFUL THINKING REMAIN UNPRODUCTIVE, See Business.

I do a little Facebook stalking. Nothing on his page. Nothing on anyone else's page who might be with him if he did come home.

It's ridiculous that I'm even checking. He said he'd let me know when he got back, and I just have to wait. I can't make him get home faster by checking my messages, right?

Besides, he's a college guy. He's probably used to girls being much more relaxed about things like this.

I can do relaxed.

150

One hour. I will put my phone down for one hour.

I make it fifteen minutes. Pathetic.

I'm trying on potential clothes for the next recreation when Ray hollers up the stairs that I've got a visitor. It can't be Sun. She'd just come upstairs, and based on the lack of footsteps coming my direction, I'm guessing it's a member of the male species. Ray is trés old school when it comes to boys in my room.

Could it possibly be Blake? I don't even know why it would be, but suddenly I'm convinced of it. My pulse races as I peel off my black recreation clothes and search for some casual, oh-this-old-thing?, sexy-yet-not-trying-too-hard mystery item of clothing that surely resides in my closet.

Turns out, there is no such mystery item hiding on a hanger.

Eventually, I settle on a sundress that is believable as something I'd wear to hang around the house on a Sunday. A quick swipe of blush and some mascara is all the make-up I'll allow myself to maintain the casual image I'm going for. There's nothing to be done about the ponytail dent in my hair, so I try to go with a loose up-do look with a few bobby pins.

By now, I'm pressing my luck with Blake's patience, I'm sure. God knows what kind of third-degree-disguised-as-small-talk Ray is subjecting him to. Not to mention the disastrous state of the living room. The last time I was down there, there were lamps piled on the couch.

God.

I run down the stairs and pull up short when I see Caine. "Oh."

"Hey," he says.

He is so not Blake. What was I even thinking? Of course Blake wouldn't show up at my house after one phone call. And now I'm wearing a dress and make-up. I blush, which makes me feel even stupider. "Hey." Then it dawns on me why he must be here. "You didn't bring the books back, did you?" I demand.

He holds up empty hands. "Do you see any books?"

"You better not have brought them back." I point my finger at him.

"Mara, you're being awfully rude," Ray says.

Caine is surveying the chaos of the living room. I imagine his inner child huddled under his inner kitchen table and crying. This has got to be a minimalist like Caine's worst nightmare. I've got to get him out of here.

"You wanna take a walk?" I ask.

He shoves his hair back, then stuffs his hands in his

pockets. "Yeah, sure."

"Great." I tap him on the elbow as I brush past to open the front door. "Come on."

He follows me across the lawn to the street. We walk on the scattered gravel in the gutter as I lead him around the corner and down toward the park, and for the ten-thousandth time, I really wish we had sidewalks in this neighborhood. We're on the opposite side of the Menomonee River from the running paths and picnic areas that everyone knows. This is my neighborhood, my stretch of woods, and I'm familiar with every inch of the uneven terrain. Caine keeps pace without any difficulty as I put some space between us and my house.

"You okay?" he asks when I finally slow down to a maintainable speed.

"Yeah, I'm fine." I give him a tight smile. "Sorry. I just go a little crazy when my mom is rearranging the house."

"Happen a lot?"

"A lot." I nod. "I fear for my room when I move out."

We talk a little bit about when we both leave (next Wednesday for me, not until the first weekend in September for him), how I don't know my roommate, and he doesn't know yet if he'll have one, how I'm nervous about the food being awful since I'm a vegetarian. Nothing that matters. A yellow-winged butterfly dances ahead of us as we walk, until it disappears into the tree line.

He asks how my photo project is coming and I end up telling him about the impossibility of recreating clown soccer.

"So, not well, then?" he says.

I blow out a sigh. "It's not...perfect."

"No one's forcing you to do this."

"Technically, no. But Sun really wants to go through with the new plan."

"Which is?"

I tell him about the super-secret plans for tomorrow. He listens quietly, shaking his head with the barest of smiles while I explain.

"I'm just not sure what this has to do with Clown Soccer," he says.

"Haven't you ever had one of those strange experiences?" I ask. "Something just totally out of place that made you suddenly stop and realize how completely weird life is?"

"Like my house burning down?" he asks with one eyebrow slightly lifted.

SURGEONS ATTEMPT RISKY SURGERY TO REMOVE LOCAL GIRL'S FOOT FROM MOUTH, See

Heath.

"I was thinking of something a little happier."

"Such as?"

"Like..." I cast around in my mind for something, reeling through four years of shared memories. "Oh! Remember when we had that assembly sophomore year—"

That's all I have to say before he laughs one of his rare his throaty laughs. "When the random cat ran across the stage? Yeah, I remember."

"See? That's exactly what I'm talking about. You knew right away. That's all I want. To make that moment happen for someone else."

"I guess." Caine stops suddenly and peers into the trees. "Is that a treehouse?"

"Yeah. Wanna see?" I step over the long grass at the edge of the trees onto the narrow paths Ray tells me are made by deer.

The mysterious treehouse is barely visible from the street, even in winter when the leaves have all fallen, but once you're past the first few trees, it's plain. An irregular shape, approximately five feet on each side, it sits only twelve feet or so off the ground, with a few boards nailed to the trunk for a ladder.

"I thought this was a public park," Caine says, staring up at the structure.

I nod. "It is. I don't know who built it, but it's been here as long as I've lived here."

"I can't believe no one's pulled it down." One of his hands floats up to the first rung of the ladder.

"You wanna go up?"

"It'll hold us?"

"Sure. I've been up there a bunch of times." Sun and I have spent hours up there over the years, with nothing but a deck of cards and cups of coffee.

He nods, blue eyes wide behind his glasses, and I can't help smiling. He gestures for me to go first, but I pinch the hem of my dress and tell him to go first instead. I'm willing to climb the tree in a dress, but not with him staring up at my pink underpants.

There are no railings and not much space up top, but we'll be able to sit side-by-side with our legs dangling over the edge. Caine can't stop looking around, like he's trying to memorize every millimeter of the view. I reach back before I remember I don't have my backpack. No backpack means no camera. I don't even have my phone with me for a quick snapshot.

"Damn," I mutter.

"What?"

"I wish I had my camera. Your face is priceless right now."

Immediately he scowls, erasing the look of wonder.

"Never mind, you ruined it."

"Thank you."

"It wasn't a compliment." I roll my eyes.

"Even better."

I give him a look and settle onto the platform beside him.

His head is back to swivel mode and his eyes are widening again, despite his best efforts. "This is weird," he says.

."This is kind of what I want to achieve tomorrow."

He leans forward to look down and his hands reflexively curl around the edge of the platform, his left hand partially covering my right in his scramble to get a grip.

"Scared?" I tease.

Straightening, he takes his hand off mine and shoves his hair out of his eyes with it. "It seems higher when you look straight down."

"After you get down to Chicago, we should go to the Willis Tower and go out on those glass platforms." I wiggle my eyebrows.

"Yeah, maybe."

I study him for a minute while he looks up at the

branches. "Are you going to completely disappear?" I ask.

"Huh?"

"When you get to DePaul. I'm never going to hear from you again, am I?"

"What makes you think that?"

"You said high school is nothing but a waiting room. You don't care if you ever see anyone ever again, do you?" I feel hollowed out at the thought. Chicago seems so far from home, and I'm kind of desperate for some kind of safety net. I'd like to know that I could call Caine some time when I'm lonely for home.

He squints at me. "You really think I'm heartless, don't you?"

"You're the one who doesn't even want his yearbooks." I kick my feet out for emphasis and one of my flip flops falls off my foot. "Oops."

We both lean forward to watch it land on the hard ground below. It looks very orange, all alone down there.

"You want me to go get it?" he offers.

"Nah." I wiggle my toes until the other shoe drops. "I'll get 'em later."

"You have nice feet," he says, which makes my toes curl up like potato bugs in the sunlight. My face goes fire hot.

"That's a weird thing to say."

"Proves I'm not heartless, though."

"Because you complimented my feet? No." I swing my legs up and to the side, leaning on one hand, with my feet hidden under the swingy skirt of my aqua-blue dress. "You could just have a foot fetish for all I know."

I expect him to dive into a game of one-ups with me, but he just rolls his eyes. "I'm not heartless. I'm just glad high school is over, okay? No more waiting for real life to start."

"This isn't real life?"

"You know what I mean."

I don't, actually, but his tone tells me to move on. "You still didn't answer my question. Are you going to forget you ever met me even though we'll both be in Chicago?"

"No." He meets my eyes and I believe him. "I already told you – I remember it all. I just don't need to hang onto a bunch of sentimental junk to remember."

"It's not junk."

"Stuff. Whatever you want to call it." He sighs and climbs to his feet, backing away from the edge. I twist to look at him as he scans the branches overhead. Then, without another word, he's climbing. The limbs narrow considerably just a few feet above the platform, but he still manages to get onto a perch above my head even after I stand to watch his progress.

"What are you doing?"

"Just looking." He loops one elbow around a branch and shields his eyes with his free hand. "What is that?"

"How should I know?"

"Come up here."

And for some reason, I do what he says, even though I'm barefoot and wearing a dress. I can't get as high as he is, but standing on a lower branch, I'm able to grab the one he's sitting on and stretch onto my toes to look in the direction he's pointing. All I see is the river a short distance away, and trees, trees, trees.

"Right there." He bends forward until our faces are almost level and uses two fingertips to lift my chin until I'm looking exactly where he's looking. "There." His breath makes the baby-fine hairs on my cheek stand on end. "It looks like there's a road in the river."

"Oh, that. There is."

"Why?" He sits up, moving away from me, and I twist to face him, rearranging my feet carefully on the rough bark of the oak tree. One of his knees pokes into the space between my extended arm and my body, and our arms cross around the back of the trunk where we're both holding on. It's very crowded up here in the tree top.

"I'm not totally sure, but my stepfather says people used to drive their cars into the river to wash them."

"Are you kidding me?" He cranes his neck, squinting through the leaves.

"My neighbor told him about it. It was way back..." I gesture over my shoulder. "Like, in the 1920s or something."

He blinks at me with a funny look. Something like flabbergasted. "Can we get closer?"

"Yeah. Come on." Climbing down is a lot trickier than going up, and Caine has to hold me by the forearm for the last trembling step to the platform.

"Don't look down," he says, so I stare up at him unblinking while my toes flail for solid ground. When I find it, and take a much-needed breath, he smiles that faint smile again. "You were totally white."

"Hey, you're the one who freaked sitting on the edge before."

"It was all a clever ruse. I'm lulling you into complacency." He follows me to the platform in a few well-placed steps and some monkey-like agility.

"Hmm. Clever, Agent Fitzgibbon." I cross my arms. "But you've revealed your plans too early. Remember my advanced counter-intelligence training."

"I never forget." He pushes his glasses up. "Now

come on, I want to see the car wash."

I go first to avoid the up-skirt view and retrieve my flip flops from the ground while Caine makes his way down the makeshift ladder.

"This way." I take the lead along the deer paths to the edge of the quietly babbling river. It seems like nothing but a wide, shallow stream here, though just a few blocks south, it's deep and rushing again. I've always liked this small section. It's like a secret.

If I look carefully, I can make out a rough path where cars could have once been able to drive straight into the river. The trees there are younger than the ones around them, and the ground a little flatter. In the river itself, however, the road is plain. Wide, concrete slabs just an inch or two under the surface of the water. They're slick with algae and weathered at the edges, but the slabs are still clear.

"Here you go," I say.

"I can't believe people actually washed their cars in a river." Caine hunkers down at the edge like a surveyor, tilting his head to new sight lines, resting his fingertips on the ground for balance when he leans too far.

"I don't know for sure if it's true." My right hand twitches to my side again, expecting to find the familiar weight of my Canon inside my backpack, but of course it's still not there. I squint, trying to memorize the look of Caine from behind, perched on the riverbank like an enthusiastic fourth grader. It would be such a nice shot.

"Damn." I don't realize I've said it aloud until he turns to look at me.

"What?"

I shake my head. "My camera. I wish I had my camera."

His mouth tugs, but stops short of smiling. "You really are addicted. You need to join Memorabiliacs Anonymous."

The end of this conversation is a foregone conclusion, so I just stick my tongue out at him.

He turns away for a moment, then asks. "Would you stand in that water?"

I look at the river. "I *have*, but..."

"I don't have any open sores, do you?"

"Gross."

"I have to stand on the road in the river. I have to." He toes his worn Vans off and steps gingerly into the shallow water. "Are you coming in?"

"Nah, I prefer to get my hepatitis from salad bars. Thanks, though." I smile sweetly.

"Come on, I want to show you something," he says, waving me in.

"What? Show me from here."

"No, I'm going to give you a gift." He reaches into his pocket.

"You shrunk the yearbooks with some kind of witch doctor magic and you've got them in your pocket." But I'm stepping out of my flip flops already.

"I prefer Voodoo. And no."

With my arms outstretched like a tightrope walker, I wade into the cool current. The old road is slimy underfoot and a little squeal escapes my lips. Caine snorts something resembling a laugh. I ease closer until we're at arm's length. "What do you want to give me?"

"Come closer." He waves an impatient hand. I place my feet carefully in the algae where the current is still disrupted by his feet.

"Okay."

He pulls his iPod out of his pocket and unwraps the headphones. "When I lost everything in the fire, there was nothing I could do to get it back."

I nod, not wanting to speak.

"But I realized something. When Christmas came around that year, my mom got a new copy of her stupid Chieftains album and when she played it, I felt like I was back in my old house." He waits for me to respond, but all I can think of to do is nod again. It seems to be enough though, because he continues. "The fire didn't burn up music. There's nothing that could make every copy of a song disappear forever."

His face is so serious, but so open, I can't stop looking at him. I've never realized what a wall he keeps up all the time. I thought I knew him, at least enough to call him a friend, but this... It takes my breath away to know I'm seeing something new. Something very few people have seen.

"Anyway...here." He holds out one of the earbuds from the headset.

I slip it into my ear while he puts the other one in his, and I wait with my stomach full of butterflies for him to start the music. I don't know why I'm nervous. But it's the good kind of nervous.

After a breath, the music starts with a throbbing bass line over a rock beat. When the keyboards come in, I recognize it, and smile. "Stars Align" by MausHaus.

The gentle babble of the of river doesn't fit with the driving rhythm of the song, but it's perfect anyway. It fits with the rhythm of my own blood, I think. I take a deep breath, wanting to pull everything inside of me.

A breeze sets the leaves and my skirt fluttering. My palms itch with an urge to move so I press them against my legs and tip my head back to look up at the clouds. The music fills my brain and I imagine it pushing the clouds along their paths across the baby blue sky. I imagine it riding the river all the way to Lake Michigan, turning heads as it floats by.

"Hold you in my arms..." the lead singer croons.

The chorus soars. I want to wrap my arms around the sky and the trees and Caine and the music and the river.

Caine puts his hand on my shoulder as he leans close to speak softly in my ear. "Now whenever you hear this song, you can think of the time you stood on a road in the middle of a river."

I nod as he pulls back, and when his hand slips from my shoulder, I catch his fingertips with mine. I don't know why I do it, except that I feel like I'm closing a circuit. Now the white wires running between our ears aren't the only connection between us. He looks me in the eyes for the long moment while the bridge of the song becomes the resonant frequency of the world, but then he drops his gaze to the rippling surface of the water. I close my eyes, focusing on the music, the feel of the water trickling over my feet, the pressure of his fingertips hooked on mine.

He's right. I will be transported here every time I hear this song from now on.

When the last chord fades from my ear, he lets go

of my hand. I pull the earbud free, closing it in my fist. I press my thumbnail against my lips, not quite ready to give up the moment, even though it's just us and the river again.

"Thank you," I say as I put the earbud in his cupped hand.

"You're welcome." He meets my eyes again, and the butterflies come back. I wonder if I'm coming down with something. My stomach is so jittery today.

The ghost of the song twirls in the space around me, and I have to do something to break the spell. He wasn't trying to enchant me, he was just playing a song for me. So I ask, "Are we done with our *e.coli* foot bath?"

"I don't know how you expect to really get infected if you don't stay in."

I laugh as I pick my way back to the bank and find a fallen log to perch on while I let my feet air dry. My flip flops are so going in a bucket of bleach when I get home. Yuck.

After a minute, Caine joins me and shoves his feet into his Vans still wet. Double yuck.

I've got goosebumps after getting my feet wet, and the warmth of his body beside me feels good. The chorus of the song rolls through my mind in waves. I can't believe he's been capturing memories with music all this time.

"Now I want to give you something," I say.

"What?"

"Will you come to Veterans' Park tomorrow? I want you to be part of the next plan."

He nods, no protest. "Yeah, sure."

"Really?" I smile at him.

"Yeah, what the hell? I'm probably going to die of some horrible bacterial infection the day after tomorrow anyway." He nods at the river.

"That's the spirit."

———

I DON'T FIND the yearbooks he left on the couch until long after he's gone.

———

FOR THE RECORD, Blake doesn't text.

[13]

THANKFULLY THE SUN is still up when Sun parks her car on Lincoln Memorial Drive. The master plan has a lot more potential to get us arrested after dark. According to the plan, we should be the first to arrive, so we quickly get the rest of our supplies out of the trunk and head into Veteran's Park. There's not a lot of trees in the park, except around the lagoon, so we hurry in that direction, hoping to be under cover before the next group of black-clad teenagers arrive.

I've got butterflies again, and they're still the good kind.

When we're safely in the stand of trees, Sun grins at me. "This is going to be awesome."

"I hope so."

We hunker down to assemble the rest of our stuff while we wait.

"I can't believe we've only got a couple more of these before we're done," she says.

"I know. Of course, everything will pale in comparison to this magnificent feat from now on, but..." I shrug.

"I prefer to think that we just have a new personal best that we can endeavor to surpass."

"Endeavor to surpass?" I repeat with a grin.

"Words aren't just for nerds anymore, baby." She lowers her Elvis sunglasses and winks at me.

"Who are you calling a nerd?" I grin.

"Hey!" someone hisses. We both turn to see Deanne, Mick, and Ruthie scooting into the protection of the trees a few yards away. We wave to them.

Over the next ten minutes, another five people arrive, Caine among them. I'm thrilled to see everyone took us seriously on the costuming. We are a sea of black in the shadows made by the copse of trees.

Sun takes over preparations. I might be the cause of this event, but this one has become Sun's baby. It appeals to all of her favorite things: theatricality, fun, and ridiculousness. She checks everyone's equipment, doles out accessories from her duffel bag for final costume prep, and reviews the entrance plan.

"All right, everybody. Let's ninja it up."

Following Sun's instructions, we all pull black t-shirts over our heads, with the neck holes exposing our faces. We tie the sleeves of the shirts behind our heads and do a little arranging to make the fronts show only our eyes. People spot-check each other, looking for stray hairs and making sure the t-shirt tags aren't showing. If it wasn't for the steady wind coming in across Lake Michigan, we'd be wilting under all this black clothing in August. Even with the wind, it's pretty hot.

I survey the group when we're all done. Do we actually look like ninjas? No, but I think it's going to be a very convincing display when we hit the open field.

Even with her mouth covered, I can tell Sun is grinning. Her eye makeup is spectacular today, a magenta color on her lids and thick black liner winging out to peaks. Since that's all I can see under her ninja mask, it looks even more striking.

"You ready for this?" she asks.

"Yep." I lift my chunky camera by its strap. It's a little bulky for a ninja, but I'm not risking bad shots. "Ready when you are."

"Okay, people, this is not a drill!" She crouches at the edge of the trees and peers out at the wide, flat field before us. "Ruthie, Deanne, you're first."

Giggling in a very un-ninja-ish way, Ruthie backs into the field, letting out string from her reel as she goes. When she's got a decent length meted out, she turns and runs, string trailing behind her. Deanne takes off a few strides later with Ruthie's blue and yellow kite held aloft in one hand. It doesn't take long for the wind to catch the diamond shape and then there are two ninjas in command of a cheerful kite in the middle of the park.

"Myra, Justin, head up to the corner before you two go." Sun points the next pair to the north and they set off through the trees. "Chris, you go."

Another ninja darts into the open field, this time pulling a two-stringed stunt kite. Sun gives the kite a toss into the wind for him, then hurries back to the trees. Fifty yards north, a very short ninja pops out of the woods followed by a tall one holding a box kite. They get it aloft and the tall one runs back to the trees.

By now, people in the park are starting to take notice. Beside me, Cori squeals with excitement. I lift the camera, wishing I had a telephoto lens. Still, I fire off a few quick shots of the four ninjas already deployed in the park. The brightly colored kites are exactly the contrast Sun and I had imagined.

"Mick, go. I'll give you a lift." Sun launches another kite, this one sporting Batman, as Mick runs into the field to join the others.

"Me next!" Cori jumps to her feet and shakes her butterfly kite at Sun.

"Okay. You and Justin go when he gets back."

Cori doesn't wait; she heads north to meet Justin and in a moment they appear running together with the butterfly trailing them.

Only Caine, Sun and I are left. Sun turns her magenta eyes on us. "Let's go!"

Sun goes first, with me giving her orange octopus kite a lift as she runs out the string. Then I come back to do the same for Caine with my own traditional rainbow-colored delta kite. He's agreed to hold the string for me so I can get some pictures.

"You ready?" I ask.

"What the hell." He shrugs, but his eyes show signs of a potential smile under his ninja mask. Can't be sure with Caine.

We dash into the clearing. My easy-flying kid's kite soars up to join the others and I feel the familiar thrill watching it rise. There is magic in kites.

The impromptu ninja kite festival is definitely attracting attention now. All around the park, people are stopping to stare and laugh. I see camera phones appearing on all sides. This is exactly what I was hoping for.

Beneath my mask, I'm smiling so big I'm probably going to have a mouthful of black t-shirt lint. I wonder if ninjas wear masks to hide the fact that they're grinning their asses off, too. It could be.

HISTORIANS AGREE: BEING A NINJA WAS AWESOME, See Lifestyle.

"Aren't you going to take any pictures?" Caine asks.

"Oh! Right!" I open the lens and try to capture the moment as best I can. I don't have time to adjust every setting with precision in a situation like this, but I make a few tweaks after the first couple shots. Luckily, the depth of field pretty much takes care of itself in this kind of light. In quick succession, I capture shots of Mick crouched low with one foot extended and his Batman kite reeling overhead, Justin helping Myra guide the box kite higher into the sky, Cori running in a dead sprint while her butterfly does loop-de-loops behind her, and a cluster of spectators staring in open-mouthed wonder.

"This is amazing!" I shout to Sun when she gets close enough to hear me.

"Keep it cool, ninja," she says.

I laugh.

"Hey, get over here," Caine says.

"You need me to take over?" I ask, reaching for the red plastic reel.

"No, but if you're going to drag me along on your adventure and enforce madcappery, you damn well better be standing next to me for it."

"You came here under your own power, Citizen Caine."

"That's what they want you to think." He flicks his eyes to either side.

"But if you actually came here under your own power, you've already beaten them at their own game," I say.

"Unless that was their goal all along."

I nod. "You can never really be sure, can you?"

"That's why I keep the lie detector in my trunk."

"I keep mine in my bra."

He laughs, a full, startled laugh that makes me join in. I don't think I've ever heard such a genuine one from him.

"Come on." Gripping the reel of string in one hand, he grabs my hand in his free one and runs across the field, pulling my kite along with us. The rainbow delta weaves between Cori's butterfly and Mick's Batman, then Caine makes a hard left to avoid crashing into Ruthie, who has her back to us. My delta starts to lose altitude and he has to let go of my hand to pull the kite back into flight.

"Nice recovery," I say.

"It's not my first time."

I decide to use my new perspective to get a few

more pictures, but Deanne runs up to stop me after a few shots.

"Don't! You'll ruin the ninja illusion."

"The pictures are the whole point, Dee."

She takes on a karate stance, then draws a flattened, blade-like hand across the horizon at chest height. "Ahhh, but tonight grasshopper...Google-fu will reveal that all these strangers' have shared their pictures of us. I predict the Ninja Kite Festival will go viral."

"Seriously?"

"The power of Instagram is strong, young Padawan." She nods sagely.

"Did you just switch from racist Kung-fu speak to Yoda?" Caine asks.

Her eyes narrow, and she says, "I'm mentally giving you the finger."

"As is the ninja code."

Suddenly I notice a man kneeling at the edge of the footpath with a big camera bag open at his knee. He pulls out a large, professional camera and screws on a lens. Right away, I want to run over to check out his equipment, but I know Sun'll kill me if I break ranks right now.

I nudge Deanne, and point out the photographer. "Go tell Sun."

Her eyes light up and she dashes across the grass.

The mystery camera man takes a few pictures. I can't stop staring. I want to see his camera. I want to have his camera.

Sun runs into my field of vision, orange octopus jiggling merrily overhead. She heads straight for Camera Man, and the rest of us follow in her wake as if tethered to her.

I fully expect my best friend to make the first move, but it's Camera Man who speaks up. "Hey, what's the story here?"

"No story," Sun says. "Just a little kite flying. It's Veteran's Park."

"I meant the ninja getups."

Sun waves Justin over and hands off the reel of her kite. Now hands free, she turns to face the guy completely and props her fists on her hips with her feet spread wide. "Even ninjas need a little fun once in a while."

"I work for the *Journal-Sentinal*. You guys okay with being in the paper?"

Sun keeps her posture stiff, and turns to face all of us. Her eyes are wide and sparkling like diamonds at this turn of events. She doesn't speak, but makes eye contact with everyone who isn't distracted by a kite. She seems to like what she finds there, because she turns back to the photographer. "We accept."

He asks if any of us want to give a name, but no one does. Instead, we go back to flying our kites while Camera Man gets a few more shots.

Then, quite suddenly, Sun decrees, "Ninjas, let's move out."

As if we'd rehearsed it, all the kite flyers start reeling in their string until the kites get low enough to either capsize or be caught by others.

"To the trees," Sun says, and we all run for the cover of the trees where we left our bags. Out of sight of the main field, she lowers the bottom of her mask to grin at the rest of us. "That was amazing. It could not have gone better!"

"What do we do now?" Ruthie asks.

"Ninjas night out?" Chris suggests.

"No." Sun is firm. "We have to leave our ninja selves here." She unties the sleeves behind her head and pulls the t-shirt off. No one says anything about the wind-tunnel look of her hair. "We'll ruin it if we do this anywhere but here."

I agree, so I take my mask off too, rubbing my face in all the places the shirt was.

"So this is it?" Deanne lowers her mask and sticks out her lip in an exaggerated pout.

"Trust me. It would lose something if we kept

going." Sun is already pulling off her long-sleeved black shirt to reveal a bright pink tank top that says *Bacon!* across the chest in rainbow letters. After rummaging in her bag, she pulls on a skirt that looks suspiciously like a pillowcase I recognize from her house, and extracts her loose black pants from underneath.

In a few minutes, we've all removed enough black clothing to blend into the crowds when we disperse. Apart from the duffel bags – and the fact we'll be creeping out of the trees – we barely look suspicious. I hope no one figures out it was us.

Once again, Sun takes charge, sending people out in all directions and with long intervals between. During one of the breaks between escapes, I stand up to wrap my arms around her.

"Thank you so much. This was unbelievable."

"We did good," she agrees, squeezing me.

"This one was all you, Sun."

"You said ninjas. That's the magic word." She shrugs. "Besides, we're gonna be in the paper!" She twists to look behind me at Caine. "How do you like that, Citizen Caine? I got you in the news for once."

"I'm just surprised it wasn't the police blotter."

Sun nods. "Me, too. So, we're going to Webb's for some tasties. You comin'?"

I hold my hands out. "I really shouldn't go. Tomorrow's my last day with the twins, and I promised I'd bring them Rice Krispie treats."

"How long does it take to melt marshmallows?" Sun says.

"A lot longer when you don't even have the supplies at home."

She scowls at me. "At least come for a little while."

"I can take you home," Caine says.

Sun lets us know how utterly lame we are, but only for a few minutes until she waves us into the park to make our exit. He had to park pretty far away, and as we walk, I can't help looking around for Camera Man. I'm paranoid he's going to recognize us somehow, even though I took off my black turtleneck. My nerves make me sweat in my black leggings.

We make it to the car without a paparazzi attack demanding the truth about our involvement in the ninja events – whew! But when I open the passenger door, hot, stale air body slams me, and sweat prickles up and down my back. Getting inside, I start to see stars.

"Air conditioning – please!" I beg, cranking dials on the console.

"It's a little slow," he says.

"As long as it's coming eventually." I roll down the

window for a breath of the lake breeze, but it's not much of an improvement.

"Eventually." He checks the mirrors and pulls into traffic. Motion helps bring a little more air into the car, but I'm still too hot. Sweat is actually beading on my upper lip. Gross.

Caine doesn't say anything for a few minutes as he navigates the busy street and oblivious pedestrians on his way to the freeway on-ramp just blocks away. Meanwhile, I close my eyes and think of Antarctica, which doesn't help at all. At a stoplight, I listen to the sound of him searching through the pocket on the door, then startle when he leans across me to open the glove compartment.

"Sorry," he mutters as he digs a CD out of the box. "Here we go." He feeds the disc into the stereo and taps through tracks.

When the song starts playing I burst out laughing. "I haven't heard this since I was a kid."

"Good. Now it can be the soundtrack to the Ninja Kite Festival." He turns up the volume as we pick up speed on the on-ramp. The wind whips up to a frenzy and I have to grab handfuls of my hair to tame it.

I smile at him and settle back into the seat to listen to the bouncy strings and strange harmonies.

"Light and Day." The name of the song comes to

me as it plays, though I can't remember the artist.

The windows roll up and I realize cool air is starting to come out of the vents. I aim all available vents at my face and breathe deep. Air conditioning rocks.

I close my eyes and let my mind fill with the images of my friends running across an open field with their kites. It was as bizarre and wonderful as I'd hoped. I am completely confident that everyone who witnessed our impromptu festival is going to remember the strange happening for the rest of their lives. The song is perfect. It reminds me of a kite looping, darting and soaring on invisible winds.

My left hand lifts off my lap a little. I want to touch Caine for some reason. Close the circuit again. As if I need a partner in this moment. That's weird, I know, so I curl my fingers tight and press my fist into the edge of the seat instead. But with my eyes closed, I feel like his presence is growing in the car. Like if I were to stretch out just my pinkie, I couldn't help but bump into him.

I have to open my eyes to check. He's right where I left him, behind the wheel with his eyes trained forward. The maxed out A/C has his dark hair frolicking on the current, and I can't resist catching a few of his curls in my fingers.

He startles and reaches up like a bug has landed on

him, finding my hand instead. He does a double-take, swerves too far to the right and slaps his hand back on the wheel. I grab the door with one hand and Caine's shoulder with the other, letting out an involuntary yelp.

"Sorry!" he says. "I thought – I just...sorry." He glances at me.

"Uh uh, buddy, you better keep all four of your eyes on the road. You're obviously a hazard." I reach over to grip his jaw to keep him facing forward, but he jerks as soon as my fingertips graze skin. "Whoa, okay. No touching, I get it."

"No, it's not that. I...you..." He shakes his head. "Sorry."

I pull my hands into my lap. "I get it. You do hard time, you get a little weird about being touched."

"I'm not weird about being touched." He shoves his elbow into my arm.

"I don't know...you're a pretty weird guy."

"You would certainly know."

I make a face at him, but let it drop in favor of watching the scenery pass for a while. Part of my brain makes a list of the things I need to make my Rice Krispie squares, while the rest of it tries not to think too much about tomorrow being my last day with the twins. They may drive me crazy sometimes, but they've been a part of my life for three years. I've watched them grow from kindergarten to second grade. I am so going to miss them.

"What's better, peanut butter or chocolate?" I ask.

"Huh?"

"Peanut butter Rice Krispie treats or the ones made with Cocoa Krispies?"

"I like the ones with the chocolate on top."

"Ah, a man of discerning taste."

"Champagne, caviar and chocolate-covered Rice Krispie treats."

"Damn it! Who told you I put caviar in my Rice Krispie treats?"

The corner of his mouth quirks up for a second. "You need a full-time chaperone."

"All right, fine. You're it."

"What?"

"You're going to help me make Rice Krispie treats."

[14]

"HELLO?" I CALL as I let us into my dark house.
There's no answer. "Guess they're out." Groping for the
wall switch, I illuminate the living room.

"Whoa." Caine steps back into the foyer and looks
around. "Is this the same house?"

I look at the living room, which is restored to
perfect order. It's rearranged, and I know I'll probably clip
my shin on the coffee table a few times over the next week,
but it's livable. "I guess my mom's almost done with this
redecoration phase."

"She works fast."

"It's not her first time."

He follows me down the hall to the kitchen, where
I drop my grocery bag on the counter.

"So where are your parents?" he asks while I turn
on lights and start unloading the bag.

"I don't know." A quick check in the usual spots
reveals no notes from Mom. "Ray probably took my mom

out to dinner to celebrate the end of the redecorating chaos."

"How often does she do this?"

I shrug. "Depends. Sometimes it's just one room. This time she wanted to do all the halls, and that meant a lot of territory was affected. I'm glad she finished, though. She's probably spent for the time being. Maybe my room will remain intact."

"You think she's going to change it?"

"I'm ninety-nine percent sure she's going to change it. She was already eying up the holes in the wall." I make squinty eyes. "I could practically see the putty knife and spackle reflected in her pupils." Cabinet after cabinet, I can't find the bowl I'm looking for. "But I've kept her out of there for four years. I knew it was a ticking time bomb."

"Does that bug you?"

"Well, I'm not thrilled, but we had a deal." Ah, there's my bowl. "And I know the way she is. Change, change, change." I stretch on my tip toes, but I still can't reach the bowl. "Could you...?" I turn to ask for help, but he's already at my side, reaching easily to the top shelf for the glass bowl.

He hands it to me, and asks, "What else do you want me to do?"

"You can melt the butter for me." My phone pings

while I'm getting out the saucepan, and I find a message from Sun.

Look what Deanne just found. The message is attached to a screenshot from Instagram. It's hard to make out on my small screen, but I recognize all the kites in the air.

"Omigosh, we're already online. Look." I hold my phone out for Caine, who pushes his glasses up and looks intently at the screen.

"That was fast."

"Maybe we will go viral. That would be crazy."

"I'm just glad you can't tell it's me."

A pang stabs me in the chest. "You didn't have to come, you know."

He sighs. "It's not that. I'm just not into being in the paper."

"Except as a by-line." I let the stick of butter drop into the saucepan.

"Right." He takes the wooden spoon I offer and pokes at the chilled stick.

I start chocolate chips melting in the microwave and help myself to a mini-marshmallow before counting out the forty I need. "What's the deal with that, anyway? Why do you want to be a reporter if you hate the past? Isn't that just writing about what already happened?"

He sighs. "For the last time. I don't hate the past. I'm fine with the past. And I want to be a reporter to make sure it gets recorded accurately. The past deserves truth, so when people look back in the future, they don't get all clouded by nostalgia."

"People like me?"

"Not just you." He jabs at the butter hard enough to shove the pan off the burner a bit. "When my house burned down, the article in the paper the next day was awful. They got my dad's name wrong, they said the fire started in the wrong room, and they didn't mention my brother's gerbils."

I've totally lost count of my marshmallows. I keep looking at him out of the corners of my eyes. He's only two feet away, but there might as well be a canyon between us. "I'm sorry."

"Please don't."

"Don't what?"

"Apologize. Feel sorry for me. This is why I don't talk about it. I just want to leave it behind."

I know I shouldn't say anything, but sometimes my mouth seems to report to a higher authority. "So, you're fine with the past as long as it's not *your* past."

His jaw works for a second while he stares intently into the saucepan. "Yeah, maybe."

"You know that's weird, right?"

"It's not weird."

"Okay, hypocritical? Counter-intuitive? Utter bullshit? What's your pleasure?"

He sticks one hand in his pocket and withdraws something, which he slaps down on the counter before me. "I would like to play this Get-Out-Of-Conversation-Free Card." When he lifts his hand, there's nothing beneath.

I pretend to pick it up and examine it. "This is clearly an I-Acknowledge-My-Own-Bullshit Card."

"Turn it over," he instructs.

I flip the imaginary card. "This side just says, I-Am-About-to-Burn-Mariska's-Butter."

He chuckles one of his throaty, soft laughs.

I step closer to turn the burner down. "That sounds rusty. You really should use it more."

"The butter?"

"Your laugh." I pop another marshmallow into my mouth and start counting the rest into the pot. There are twenty in the pot when he takes two out to eat them. "Hey! You're going to screw up my count."

He rolls his eyes and reaches across me to fish two out of the bag. "Happy?"

"Deeply and consistently." Leaving him to stir the marshmallows into a gooey slop, I measure out peanut butter and stand at the ready with the metal scoop, watching the saucepan for signs of burning.

"Do you think you got the pictures you were hoping for tonight?" Caine asks.

"I don't know. I hope so." The saucepan looks just right, so I yank it off the burner and use my finger to scrape the peanut butter into the mess. "Keep stirring." I dump Rice Krispies into a bowl without measuring – I've done this a million times and the entire box does just fine – and wave Caine over with the pan. "Pour."

He does while I begin the arduous task of mixing the two together.

"Did you at least do what you set out to do?"

My spoon slows without my permission as I look at him. "I really think we did. I mean, it's definitely not the same being the ones putting on the show, but...I'm happy."

He squints at me, then shakes his head. "I have to say, I wouldn't do all this myself, but I admire your dedication."

"Why do I feel so patronized?"

He shrugs. "That's something you'll have to discuss with your psychiatrist."

"I'll tell him you said hello."

We don't talk except for a few murmured instructions as I scrape the sloppy concoction into a pan and pour melted chocolate over the top. Caine scoops up some chocolate with one finger and makes a "Hm!" sound of surprise at the temperature, stuffing his finger into his mouth.

"That's what you get for sticking your finger in my Rice Krispie treats."

"You say that to all the guys." His finger is still in his mouth, making his words garbled, but still understandable.

"No, I just take them up to my room."

The finger slides out and hovers not far from his mouth. "Wha—?"

I laugh. "Oh my God, Caine, you need to relax." I tap on the edge of the glass pan, still steaming slightly. "These have to cool. Let's go look at the pictures from today."

"Oh." His hovering hand disappears into his hair. "Yeah, sure."

"Come on." I lick a smudge of chocolate off my thumb and grab my backpack from the table as I lead Caine through the pristine living room to the not-even-slightly-pristine hall where there are random pieces of my parents' bedroom lining the wall. Obviously, Mom has moved on to their bedroom. "Guess she's not done after all. Sorry about the mess," I say, remembering Caine's careful effort to prevent me from seeing his brother's room.

"You weren't kidding about this."

"My room's not much better right now." I flick the light on, and gesture for him to go in. "It's kind of a work in progress."

He stares at the piles, boxes, and my unmade bed. Oh God, why didn't I make my bed today?

"Sorry...it's...I was kind of busy with the ninja thing..." I drop my backpack on the desk chair and hastily yank the blankets up to cover my striped sheets.

"Don't worry. If the EPA comes for my brother, I won't mention your name."

"It's not that bad." But it totally is. It's not messy, really, just disorganized. It's not like I have dirty dishes piled everywhere.

"It's not what I expected." He turns in a circle, as if there's something he's missed. "I figured you'd have pictures all over."

"You obviously didn't look close enough at the walls."

I take a seat at the desk to connect the camera to my laptop, and Caine squeezes between two laundry baskets to peer at the wall. "Oh yeah." He covers a pinhole with a fingertip. "Wow, there was stuff all over."

"Yeah. Here, I probably have a picture of it somewhere." A scroll through my newly expanded library yields quick results. "There." I've found a picture of Anna standing on my desk chair with her hands clamped to her sides and her serious face tilted slightly up. She was being an Academy Award. Long story.

He bends low over my shoulder to look at the screen. "Whoa."

Behind Anna, the walls look like a cluttered museum, or the wall at one of those family restaurants with old stuff from the '50s all over. "I guess it's a little much."

"No, it's very you."

My face feels hot on the side where he hovers close. "My future roommate will no doubt be grateful I can't recreate this in our dorm room, huh?"

"She'll just have to look at ninjas flying kites instead." He straightens, then hunkers down beside my chair. "Let's see what you've got."

I surf back to the recent downloads section to look at this evening's photos. There are a lot. Switching to full-screen, I start a slide show. We watch quietly for a few minutes as ninjas of every shape and size pause on the screen mid-action. The kites photographed beautifully – even Mick's cheap plastic Batman.

"You're really good," Caine says finally. "Even running around with a mask covering your face, these are better than most people could take with the best camera in the world."

"Thanks." Glancing away from the screen, I find him looking at me.

He does his hair shoving thing, and looks back at the screen in time to see a still of himself leaning back into the wind with his feet spread and the rainbow kite giving a good fight in the upper right corner of the shot.

"That's a good one," I say.

"We'll call it 'Ninja with Rainbow.'"

"I'll hang it next to 'Bicycle Cop and the Pajama Gang.'"

"What?" He peeks at me over the top of his glasses. His eyes are much bluer without the reflection off his lenses.

"I'll show you." As I look for the pictures of me and the girls at the park, I realize Caine is shifting from foot to foot and grimacing. "Here, grab some chair." I scoot to one side and pat what's left of the seat. He hitches his hip onto the spot and leans toward the screen.

I end up going through all the pictures I've created since the beginning of the project. He studies them as if they are fine art, which makes me smile at the back of his head. I've seen him lean into the screen like this to edit, and I can't help wondering if he's finding flaws in the images.

"You're going to keep doing this, right?" He turns

suddenly, looking at me over his shoulder. Our proximity on the chair makes it hard to focus on him for a second.

"I thought you were against this whole plan."

"Not that. This." He points to the screen. "Photography."

"Oh."

He raises his eyebrows to remind me to answer.

I nod slowly. "I don't think I could ever stop."

The left corner of his mouth does that little half-smile of his, while his eyes do the rest of the job. I can't help it, I'm really growing to like that smile. I've known him for four years, but I think I could count, without taking off my socks, the number of times I saw him laugh before last week. Now, it's like I've found the secret to unlocking him. And I like that I've got that power.

His eyes drift down. I think he's looking at my mouth. Right away, I'm convinced I've got chocolate on my lips from the Rice Krispie treats. I lick my lips and he does the same.

Now I'm not so sure I've got something on my face.

Suddenly my heart is beating in my ears and I'm inexplicably dizzy. I try to swallow, but my throat is dry.

Then, he looks away and I am left breathless and confused. Was he thinking of kissing me? I feel like he was. And I'm not sure I would have stopped him.

Which is insane.

What about Blake?

But I must have imagined it, because now he's looking at the screen again as if time didn't stop just a second ago. I take a deep breath and imagine the oxygen smoothing my nerves. I am obviously still riding the high of our ninja success. Everything is fine.

"Are you going to take O'Neill up on his offer?" he asks, confirming my suspicions that I am the only one having crazy almost-kissing thoughts.

"To get some of my pictures from the paper? Yeah. I'm actually going to go over after I'm done at work tomorrow."

"I'll probably see you there."

"Yeah?" I like the idea that he'll be at school. It will be nice to have someone to talk to while I dig through back issues.

"I'm reviewing the proof for him tomorrow, and then I'm done." He lets out a relieved sigh. "Thank God."

"It's really cool you did this for O'Neill."

He shakes his head. "I'm just a sucker. I can't say no when someone asks me directly for a favor."

"You should definitely not have told me that."

Eyes narrowed slightly, he asks, "Why?"

"Because now I'm going to ask you to come to my

prom thing on Saturday night."

"I didn't even go to the actual prom."

"Isn't it lucky you get a second chance, then?"

"You have a strange definition of lucky."

"Are you saying no?" I ask.

He shifts uncomfortably in the chair, ultimately easing out of it and standing beside me. "Are you actually asking me?"

Standing, I tilt my head and lean to the left until I can see his eyes. "Caine, will you come to pseudo-prom on Saturday night?"

He sighs and looks up at the ceiling. "Yes."

"Yay!" I cheer in a tiny voice with little fist shakes to match. "Now I'll even let you eat one of my Rice Krispie treats."

The ghost of his smile appears again. "The things I will do for delicious peanut butter treats."

"That's what it says on the bathroom wall." I grin. "Right between *Jesus loves you* and *Tisha Ballestreri is a bitch.*"

"And to think I crossed out all the stuff they wrote about you." He shakes his head.

I shrug. "Why bother? It's all true, you know."

That earns me the ghost of a smile again and my heart squeezes with pleasure. I wish I'd known him this way before there was nothing but a handful of days left before I leave.

[15]

RICE KRISPIE TREATS are insufficient balm to my soul when I have to leave Maddie and Liv the following afternoon. Since July I've known this would be my last day with them, but it still hurts. More than I thought it would.

I can't stop giving them last hugs, last kisses on their blond heads, final promises to send e-mails and visit when I come home for the weekend.

"We don't want to go to Grandma's house!" Liv wails.

"We want to stay with you," Maddie says.

"I know." I hug them both, getting wet spots on both shoulders from their tears. "I want you to stay, too."

"Don't go to Chicago." Maddie almost chokes me with an extra squeeze.

I can't think of what to say to her. It's ridiculous how much I want to tell this eight-year-old girl I'll stay. Part of me wants to stay. It's not even a small part. I want everyone to stay where they are right now, and not go to college, and for everything to stay just the way it is. The thought of starting all over again as a freshman at Loyola makes me want to crawl under my unmade bed and never come out again.

"Girls, girls," Mrs. LaPierre says. "You will see Mariska again. She's not going to Mars, for heaven's sake."

But I'm crying now too, and I'm pretty sure it's not going to stop anytime soon. This is one of those situations where I'm just going to have to leave them in tears, I think.

My right knee aches from being on the edge of the sidewalk, but the girls aren't letting up. I hug them and snivel and try not to let snot drip out of my nose until Mrs. LaPierre finally puts a hand on each of the twins' shoulders and forces them to ease up.

"All right, enough now," is what she says to them, but when I look up at her, she's got tears in her eyes too. She gestures for me to stand and gives me a big hug of her own. "I don't know what we're going to do without you," she whispers so the girls can't hear.

"I'll miss you." I hug her back, remembering how much she used to intimidate me when I was sixteen in my first summer with the twins. I never would have believed we'd be clinging to each other like this.

It takes a while, but I finally get myself under control enough to give a final round of hugs and kisses to all the LaPierres and escape to my car where I can hide behind my sunglasses and a watery smile while I wave goodbye.

I shouldn't go to school now, but I do, crying along with the radio all the way. Mr. O'Neill isn't going to know what to do with me. I find the side entrance open when I arrive and try all the bathrooms along the way until I find the main girls' restroom open on the second floor. A little cold water on my face helps, but definitely doesn't cure my puffy, red face. And now I have a headache, which is awesome.

At least the tears aren't actively running down my cheeks anymore. It's probably the best I can hope for. I make my way down to Mr. O'Neill's classroom, where I find him sitting behind his desk with several stacks of paper and a stapler.

"What happened to you, Bokori?" he asks when I tap on the open door.

Explaining brings fresh tears, of course, but it's not as bad as I expected. He's really nice about it too, patting my shoulder and offering me some Kleenex.

"You're here about your pictures, right?" he asks when I've reached a lull.

"Yeah, if it's still okay."

He makes a dismissive gesture. "No skin off my

nose. You're going to have to develop the negatives yourself if there's anything you want. Fitzgibbon's got my key ring. I think the darkroom key is the one with the green ring on it."

I thank him and go down the hall to the J-room. For once, Caine isn't in front of a computer screen, though he's still got his earphones in. He's standing at one of the work tables looking at the final proof of the paper before it goes to the printer. He looks up when I enter and right away his editor face dissolves into confused concern.

"You okay?" he asks, too loudly with the music drowning out his volume sense.

I nod, then shake my head as his concern triggers more tears.

He approaches slowly, like I'm a deer in the woods, and puts one hand on my shoulder like he did while we stood in the river. Right at this second, I need more than that, so I step into him and wrap my arms around his waist, pressing my wet cheek into his shoulder. His arms land lightly on my back, like sparrows, and gradually settle into a semblance of a hug.

He smells like the J-room and heat. Ink, paper, and ozone with an undercurrent of sticky, summer skin and one of those antiperspirants with action-y names like *Rush* or *Energy*. I can tell I'm making him uncomfortable at first, but before I can pull myself together to back off, the tension in his torso releases and he hugs me a little tighter. I sigh with relief.

"What's wrong?" he asks, still a little too loud.

"I just had to leave the twins for the last time." I free one hand to wipe my nose before I can snot up his shirt, and I end up swiping my fingers on my jean shorts.

When he lets go of me, I can tell it's to see my face, not to escape my unwanted hug. He backs up to sit on the edge of one of the tables and pulls his earphones free.

"Do you need to, like, talk about it?"

I force a smile. "That's okay. It's not much to tell. I'm just...sad."

"Seems reasonable."

Which is a strange thing to say, but somehow it helps. "Thanks." I wipe the tears from beneath my eyes and try on a more authentic smile. "I can't believe how much I'm going to miss those little punks."

"You should send them pictures of your new life in Chicago."

I blink in surprise. "That's actually a really good idea."

"I have been known to have them once in a while."

"And here I thought you slept your way to salutatorian."

"Don't believe everything you read."

"Oh, I don't." I wipe my eyes again and take a post-crying deep breath. "Sorry I kind of attacked you."

"S'okay." He shrugs. "You here for your pictures?"

"No, I just really like hanging out in empty school buildings in my free time."

"Me, too."

It doesn't take too long to go through the negatives. I'd had a mental image of painstaking hours, but in reality, I'd only been on the paper for two years, and with only two issues a month during the school year, I only have two smallish file boxes to look through. Still, negatives are never easy to see, and I end up kneeling on one of the computer tables to hold the strips up to the window as an impromptu light box. You'd think there would be a light box in the J-room, but everyone else works with digital cameras.

I end up with six pictures I want to develop. "O'Neill said you have the keys to the darkroom?" I look at Caine over my shoulder from my perch at the window. He's still bent over the proof with a blue pencil in one hand.

"If he says so."

I bite my lip, hesitating. "Would you – would come down to the basement with me? This empty building kind of freaks me out."

That earns me the mini-smile. "Yeah, sure."

Our footsteps ring off the painted cinderblock walls as we descend to the lowest level. The darkroom is past the mechanical room where the unlit boiler still makes dripping, ghostly sounds. Goosebumps race up my legs, despite the heat. With a wall-jarring thud, some unseen machine chugs to life and I quicken my pace.

At last, we reach the locked darkroom and Caine starts trying keys. It is not the one with the green ring, but he gets lucky on the fifth try. The door is still in desperate need of WD-40, just as I remember it. Of all the noises in the basement, this is the first one I find comforting. Still, I can't resist opening the door wide and squinting in the direction of the light switches before I turn on the overheads. I have a fear of touching a centipede or some other creepy crawly when I have to reach for a light switch in the dark.

With the fluorescents on, the darkroom has an abandoned look. The fixtures were never meant for the glare of full-spectrum light. The long, stainless steel troughs are spotty, the dry lines look saggy overhead, the shelves of chemicals are disorderly and rusted at the corners. The poor darkroom is like a body in the morgue like this. I want to switch to the more forgiving red safety light she deserves, but first I have to set up the chemical baths.

My body goes on autopilot for this part, donning an apron and gloves to pour out the four pans of chemicals and the rinse tubs between, checking my favorite enlarger, checking the paper supply, using rubbing alcohol and cotton pads to clean the negatives I've selected. I load the negatives into separate holders. It's nice to have all the equipment to myself for once. I don't realize I'm humming along with Caine's dangling earphones until I stop to ask him if he wants to stay in with me while I make my prints.

"Yeah, sure. I've never seen how this works."

I smile, but hold up a warning finger. "You can't leave once I get started or you'll mess up my prints. Got it?"

He nods and pushes his glasses up.

"Then I'm going dark." I kill the overheads and switch on the dim red bulbs on either side of the room. Suddenly the room seems smaller and warmer, and the darkness crawls onto my skin like it's afraid of itself. Caine's music seems louder in the dark, reminding me of the tinny sound of Ray's ancient silver radio that he uses to listen to baseball games while he's working in the garage.

I work quickly, opening the f-stop and murmuring my eight-count to myself as I expose the paper. I feel Caine come closer while the light of the enlarger is on.

"I don't see anything," he says when I pull the paper off the easel.

"Not yet." I take the paper to the fresh pan of developer. "Watch." He joins me at the row of basins. Using tongs, I tap the paper under the surface of the bath, then tilt the pan back and forth, sloshing the solution over the paper.

Before our eyes, the image appears. Caine crowds closer to me. "Oh!" His genuine surprise makes me smile.

"I know," I say softly. Something about the darkroom makes me use a church voice. When the print is dark enough, I use the tongs to retrieve it and set it in my first water bath. It's not strictly necessary, but years of sharing chemicals with my classmates has taught me every trick in the book to preserve their life.

Caine sticks with me all down the trough as I bathe the paper in stop bath, fixer and hypo clear. He doesn't say anything, but I can tell from the unsteady sound of his breath and the tension in his arm where it rests against mine: he is fascinated. When I go back to the enlarger for the next mounted negative, he's like my shadow in the dark, and I can't help laughing.

"It's like magic, isn't it?" I ask.

"Mmm," is all he answers, but it's a positive sound. The music rattling out of his loose earphones changes and I think I recognize a new song I've been hearing on the radio lately. "Don't you have a speaker on that thing?"

"Huh? Oh...yeah, sure." He yanks the headphone jack loose and the sound quality improves dramatically. It's no high-quality stereo, but at least it's not filtered through the tiny diaphragms of his earbuds.

"I like this song." I shut off the enlarger and take the freshly exposed paper to the chemical trays. "Here comes the best part again."

He trips into me in the dark, and grips my hips to catch himself. For those brief seconds it's like he's slipped inside the blanket of darkness with me. As if we are children with a flashlight, hiding beneath the sheets. I'm surprised at how warm his hands are, even through the vinyl apron I wear.

"Sorry," he whispers, stepping back.

"You won't be able to see back there," I caution, holding the paper just above the developer.

He doesn't answer, but comes close again. Close enough to feel his breath on my neck. I drop the sheet into the developer and we lean forward in one motion to peer into the basin by the dim light of the red bulbs.

Over and over we make the trek from the enlarger to the baths, watching each photo swim into life. I never get tired of the magic. It always gives me shivers. Pleasant shivers, like an unexpected compliment. Everything is magnified this time, showing it to a newbie. I love how the process has him rapt.

Finally, I'm down to my last negative. It's hard to make out in the glow of the enlarger, and I find myself biting my lip as I feed it into the developing bath. I hope it turns out. Did I pick the right one? It's been a while since I saw the original.

"What is it?" Caine asks softly.

I watch the image solidify and smile to myself. This is the right one. "It's from last year. That's Valerie Gibb with the ribbon she won for her chicken at the State Fair."

"Why did you want a picture of a chicken ribbon?" He steps back slightly as I transfer the image to the water bath.

"It's not the ribbon." I turn slightly to look at him in the red glow. It's amazing how your eyes adjust to any level of light. I can make out the print on his t-shirt and the look of curiosity on his face. There's no judgment there. I like how genuinely curious he is. "When you see it in the light, you'll see. She's so happy. Valerie doesn't even make eye contact with a lot of people, but she is so proud of herself, she's practically glowing. I love that I got to be the one to catch that moment. I love this picture." I look away long enough to move it to the stop bath, and when I look back, he's staring at me in that way of his. "What?"

"You're making things really hard for me lately."

I feel like I've been hit in the stomach. "What? Why?" My hands shake when I make the transfer to the fixer.

"I was this close—" he holds up two pinched fingers, "—this close to making a clean break from all this, and then you come along with your ninjas and your magic darkroom..."

It's hard to get enough breath to speak. "I've known you since we were freshmen, Caine. What are you talking about?"

"Your picture..." He waves a hand at the line of chemical baths and looks away.

Heart in my throat, I finish treating the photo and move it to the dry line. My fingers can barely find the clothespins, much less pinch them. The darkness seems cavernous around me now. The floor, ceiling, and walls rush away from me and I am lost in the middle of nothingness with only my pounding pulse for company.

Then he's on the other side of the line, reaching up to fix the wet paper in place for me. The photo hangs between us, so I can't get even the red-tinted look in his eyes that might calm my rattled nerves. We're close enough that I sense him move even before he touches my elbow.

All at once my brain starts bailing out thoughts like I'm in a sinking rowboat. My breath, the itchiness of the apron against my legs, a beautiful coral-colored dress I had when I was nine, the smell of my grandmother's lotion, root beer-flavored lip gloss, and how much I like the word *inexorable*...

Then he ducks around the wet print so we're face-to-face with only inches between us. I can see his eyes now, but it doesn't help.

"You make me want to remember," he whispers. My pulse reaches the speed of sound as the tip of his nose nuzzles into mine. "You make me wonder if I've been wrong." Our lips touch – not a kiss, but no accident. Every part of me goes still, waiting and wanting more, until he presses his lips into mine.

I close my eyes while my mind finds energy for one last thought – *I guess he did want to kiss me yesterday* – before it abdicates to sensation. And there is plenty of that to go around. His warm hands on my shoulders, one sliding up to rest on the side of my throat. That familiar J-room smell again and the surprising softness of his lips.

He's just enough taller than me to make his hair fall forward and tickle my cheek. I push his hair away with one hand, loving the way the curls feel so light between my fingers.

The hand not resting on my neck moves down to wrap around my waist and my arm goes around his shoulders.

Melting. That's what I feel like I'm doing. Melting. Or maybe the very iron in my blood is pulling toward him, because he is a magnet. I feel...charged. Relieved. Unwound. He has the softest, gentlest lips. Like I'm slipping into a warm bath.

Then suddenly he pulls back and I gasp, nearly losing my balance. When did I go on tiptoe?

"Wha—?" I don't know what to say.

"I'm sorry," he says.

"What do you—?"

He's already shaking his head. "No, no. I'm sorry. I shouldn't have..." He clears his throat and stuffs his hands in his pockets. "Do you still need the lights off?"

That's not what I expected him to say. "Um, no. No, these should dry overnight. I'll have to come back...."

"Yeah, sure." He moves quickly to the darkroom door and fumbles for the knob. "If you set the lock on the knob it'll lock behind you." He looks back at me, still frozen under the drying lines. "I—I guess I'll see you around maybe."

"Caine, wait—" I cross the room, taking off my apron as I walk, but he's already backing into the hall. "Did I do something wrong?"

Reaching for him makes him take two more steps back.

"It's fine. Really. It's better this way." He shoves his hair back with an intake of breath like he wants to say more, but then he just shakes his head. "See ya."

"See ya..." I clutch the doorjamb, feeling confused and embarrassed, and maybe a little angry? I can't even tell.

When I hear the distant report of the firebar as Caine goes into the stairwell, I let out a squeaky sob I didn't realize I was holding in.

[16]

My Canon and I have a date. There's one recreation I have to do all by myself. It's the easiest of the list and I could have found someone to come with me, but I kind of wanted to do it alone. This is the only one that involves more than one picture.

It was an assignment for photography class originally, but it had become something of a habit for me. One of the reasons I carried my camera everywhere. The goal was to photograph a landmark or historic building, and I'd chosen a local theater that dated back to the Vaudeville era. It was called the Paradise, and it was in the middle of a block of business, distinguishable as a theater only by the marquee on the overhang. The architectural details were lovely, though, and I'd been happy with the result. Happy enough that I kept a lookout for other theaters in the area for years afterwards.

My collection was small, only seven pictures, but I want them back.

I'm glad to have this Tuesday morning to do this photo essay. There shouldn't be too much traffic to get between my camera and my subjects once everyone is at work. I start out at nine, wanting to get the best of the daylight.

The traffic is pretty light, as I hoped. I cruise with music cranked up and singing along for all I'm worth so I don't think too much about what happened yesterday between me and Caine. He obviously wants to forget it, so I should do the same.

It's working, sort of, until the car in front of me starts to roll through an intersection, then hits the brakes, making me do the same – hard. From the backseat, I hear a thump, and when I can safely check, I find the infamous yearbooks on the floor. The rear passenger door lock is broken and it's permanently open, which is why I don't keep anything in my car. But how did he know that? And when did he have time to put them in here?

"Damn it, Caine," I mutter, and turn up the volume a little louder.

———

THE FIRST FOUR pictures go well. But when I arrive at the site of the old drive-in, my heart sinks. A year ago, the old *Entrance* sign stood beside a weed-clotted gravel drive. It was missing light bulbs, and rusted straight through in places, which was exactly what I liked about it. Better still, I was able to frame the shot so the rusty sign was in the lower left third of the picture and the decaying screen, two-hundred yards back, filled the center and upper right. The screen had suffered through years of neglect, wind, and determined nest-building by birds. It was like a backdrop in a post-apocalyptic movie and I loved it fiercely.

Truth be told, I was afraid to get too close to it. It seemed like just the place a psycho killer would hide out, or at least a rabid dog. But the view from the access road was stunning.

Today, there's nothing but an excavation site and a bunch of construction workers piloting equipment. Not far from the place I'm certain the *Entrance* sign used to be, there's a plywood billboard with an artist's rendering of a dull, red brick office park and the words *Coming Soon* over one corner.

I pull my car to the side of the frontage road and get out. My chin is trembling. I feel like I've been hit in the stomach.

It's gone.

The beautiful, abandoned Starlight Drive-In is gone.

For a stupid office park.

I slump against the fender and sink to sit in the dirt. My eyes burn, and I realize I'm not blinking. I can't stop staring at the overturned earth and the still yellow hulks of the excavators and bulldozers. Here and there, a determined patch of weeds and wildflowers reminds me of the field that filled this space last time I was here. But there's no sign of the screen, the ticket booths, or the old concession stand.

Of course, I should have seen this coming. This was the one thing on my list I had a prayer of actually duplicating. Theaters don't go to music camp for the summer. Theaters don't look older three years later. Theaters don't graduate from high school and move away. But theaters get demolished. And now I can never officially cross this off my List of the Lost. It's gone.

Propping my elbows on my knees, I bury my head in my arms and let the hot tears come. This quest of mine is stupid. I'll never be able to get back what I lost. I'll never get back my past. My life.

Tears drip off the end of my nose into the dusty ground. I watch an ant divert his path to circle around the wet spots. The sun is getting high in the sky now, burning off the light cloud cover that made this morning so pleasant. Heat bears down on my shoulders and the back of my neck. I don't want another sunburn, so I guess I should move, but it seems really hard right now.

I dig in my backpack until I find my phone and take a rough picture of the desolation before me. I send it to Sun with the caption, *The Starlight Drive-In's grave.*

Nothing comes back for a few minutes while I listen to the cicadas and the rumble of the freeway in the distance. On the frontage road, a car goes by, slowing to check out the girl sitting on the ground by her car, and I have a strong feeling a squad car will be making a pass through here in a few minutes. After my run-in with Officer Davies, I suspect I'd be pushing my luck on another encounter with the police, so I push off the ground, dusting gravel from my palms and butt when I'm on my feet. My phone chirps and I find a picture of Sun's hand giving a thumbs-down. *Dislike* it says.

Maybe I should just give up on this. The pictures are gone. I type my reply behind the wheel while I wait for the A/C to kick in.

Give up if you want, but we're still going through with Pseudo Prom. Everyone's already agreed.

I half-sigh, half-laugh to myself. I could have predicted that.

Before I can answer her, I get a follow-up message. *Seriously, though, don't quit. You'll regret it.*

She's obviously not going to let me get away with it, but sometimes, a girl just needs a little sympathy.

Maybe I'll see if Alea's working at the coffee shop.

—————

WHEN I GET home with my iced soy latte, my mom is scrubbing the stove and Blake still hasn't sent me anything. I would love to say I'm not disappointed – about Blake, not my mom – but that would be a lie. I force myself to leave my phone in my backpack while I get some lunch, even though the pull of it is almost magnetic.

He's going to text today, I can feel it.

Apparently, I've become the kind of person who feels things.

Mom looks up when I drop my backpack on a chair. She looks pissed. Right away, I'm wondering what I did wrong.

I decide to go neutral. "Hi."

She flicks her head and takes a moment to cover up her irritation. "Mara."

"You okay?" I ask.

Her eyes close briefly. "I just don't understand how he gets jelly on the burners. What is he *doing* in here when he makes his breakfast?"

I press my lips tight to avoid laughing. I've heard this from her in various forms for years. Ray is a messy cook, and he seems blind to the crumbs, smears, and fingerprints he leaves behind. One of these days, I think my mom might beat him to death with a bottle of Clorox Multi-Surface Kitchen Spray. "Sorry," I say.

"You didn't do it, did you?" she mutters, bending to the task again.

I creep around her to the refrigerator in search of yogurt and a nectarine.

"There's only three blackberry yogurts left," I say. "Want me to put it on the list?" Glancing up at the freezer door, I notice the magnetized list looks shorter than usual.

"How many are you going to eat?" she asks, looking over her shoulder.

"I don't know."

"Well, you're the only one who likes that flavor, so do you think you can make do with just the three?"

Huh?

I must look confused, because she continues, "You're leaving next week, Mara." Her tone has lost all its jelly-induced edge.

"Oh. Right."

She gives a little half-smile. "Did you forget?"

"I guess I did." Suddenly I feel like crying. "I've

been so busy...."

She nods, looking away again.

I peel back the foil lid on my yogurt cup and slide onto one of the stools on the other side of the peninsula. We don't talk for a few minutes while I spoon purple yogurt into my mouth.

PEOPLE WHO DON'T LIKE BLACKBERRY HARVEST YOGURT ARE WRONG, see Food & Wine.

When she finishes scouring the jellified burner, she does a cursory wipe-down of the rest of the area and straightens up with a sigh. As she turns to rest her hip against the counter, a strand of her blond hair escapes from behind one ear. We have the same hair color, though you wouldn't know it from all the highlights she's been adding since she started to go gray. We look a lot alike, actually. Almost spooky alike. Sometimes I wonder if a woman can will a man's DNA out of her kid if she tries hard enough.

"How'd it go this morning?" she asks.

I shrug. "They tore the Starlight down."

She nods. "Oh yeah...I read something about that in the paper last year, now that you mention it."

"So, I guess that one's gone forever."

"Sorry, sweetie."

"Really?" I can't help the sarcastic tone in my voice, even though I know I'm just picking a fight.

She winces. "Of course I'm sorry. Why are you so determined to make me your enemy on this?"

"Because you wouldn't care at all if you lost a bunch of photos and cards and stuff. You don't keep any of that stuff."

"That doesn't mean I don't care."

"You don't understand."

"Then help me."

My stomach is seriously regretting the yogurt suddenly. "Some of the stuff in there was irreplaceable. And I'm tired of everyone telling me I've still got my memories, because I don't, okay? I had one picture of my father – one. And it's gone now. Forever."

"Mariska," she starts gently.

"Forget it." I shove away from the counter, leaving my tipped cup and spoon behind, to run for my bedroom.

My ruined sanctuary. There is nowhere I can go that's the same anymore.

Crawling onto my bed, I pull Yanya into my arms and ignore the inevitable knock on the door. She doesn't try again. She probably doesn't want to. There is one topic that has always been strictly taboo between us and it is my biological father.

Here are the things I know about him:

1. He was tall, with dark hair and dark eyes. At

least that's what my mom remembers.

2. He was an artist from Arizona who used metal from the junkyard to make sculptures.

3. My mother never saw him again, and never tried to contact him after she found out she was pregnant.

4. He goes by the name The Limit. Or at least he did eighteen years ago.

When I was younger, I used to imagine that someday he'd find out about me. I didn't know how, and I didn't really care. I just imagined him showing up on the sidewalk one day and holding his arms out to me with a smile.

"Mariska, I'm your father," he'd say, and maybe a tear would glisten in one eye.

That fairytale fantasy lasted until I was about ten. I couldn't tell you exactly what shattered my delusion, but I came to realize there was no conceivable way he'd mysteriously find out about me. My mother was the only possible source for that key piece of information and she wasn't even interested in finding him.

Apart from the occasional Google search for "The Limit," I never did much looking for him. There was even less to go on for me than if I'd been adopted. At least there are records of that sort of thing. Even Sun knew that her mother had left her outside a church in Korea. I had my mother's description of a mushroom-fueled night with a sexy metal-working artist at Burning Man and a birth certificate that read "Unknown" in the father spot.

The one picture I'd had of him was a poorly lit snapshot of a dark-haired guy with no shirt on and goggles hanging loose around his neck. He was tattooed and didn't smile as he stood beside my mother in the crowd at a performance art show.

Now I had nothing.

I type "The Limit artist metal sculpture" into Google and click Go without much hope. It's the first time I've bothered to add anything behind his artist name and shockingly, the fourth entry down the list is a Wikipedia page. The results show all my search terms bolded. I stiffen in my chair and feel my throat clog as I stare at the results.

__Chad Donoughue__, a.k.a. __The Limit__, (born November 11, 1966, in San Bernadino, CA, USA) is an American sculptor best known for his abstract __sculptures__ incorporating junk automotive parts. Donoughue was raised in California, but moved to Portland, OR at the age of 19 to pursue his interest in the music industry.

Donoughue began his artistic career out of a desire to construct musical instruments out of scrap __metal__. His work in scrap led him inevitably to an interest in spare auto parts and this medium has made up the main body of his work.

*Working under the professional moniker **The Limit**, Donoughue has exhibited his art around the world. He frequently demonstrates his self-taught process at festivals and art shows.*

Donoughue is best known for his piece Interrogative 3, on display at Portland International Airport. His art has also been featured in international collections including...

The article continues with a litany of museums, some I have heard of, most I haven't.

This is my father. Not The Limit, but Chad Donoughue. Chad. Of all the names I'd imagined he might have, Chad had never even occurred to me. It's...kind of drippy somehow.

My hands are shaking when I curl them into my lap. I cannot believe after eighteen years, it only took me a simple search to find the man who helped create me.

The article doesn't have a picture of him included, but it has to be him. How many metal-working artists can there be in the world who go by such a pretentious name? I can't believe he's actually successful. Frankly, with such a stupid name, I'd always assumed he was one of those people who thought he was way more impressive than he actually was. Is. He's an is. A real, live, breathing person who lives in Portland, Oregon.

I feel kind of sick and I'm not sure why.

Raising one jittery hand to the touch pad, I sweep to the bottom of the entry, wondering if there's anything I missed. There is only one source listed at the bottom of the page – his own website. I swallow the lump in my throat and click the hyperlink.

The page is black and professional-looking, with sleek photographs of hulking metal sculptures. There are links to multiple galleries, sorted by size and media. There is a longer biography and a link to contact him by email, which I quickly click away from.

I can only imagine how that message would go:

Hi, You don't know me, but 18 years ago you hooked up with a woman at Burning Man and I'm your daughter.

Yeah, no.

The last link is *Appearances*. I look at it for the sake of completeness. It's a bit out of date, with events listed as far back at March of this year. But partway down the page, I find August and on today's date, the page says "Ann Arbor Street Art Fair."

Ann Arbor, Michigan, is the town where the University of Michigan is. A town conveniently located just over five hours away from me, according to the Google maps search I just did.

Five hours.

It's not really that far, all things considered.

It could very well be the closest I've ever been to my own father. Another look at the Appearances list on his website proves it's the closest he's been this year.

I chew my lip for a minute, trying to pretend that my pounding heart hasn't already gotten the secret news from my brain.

I take a screenshot of the Google map and send a message to Sun. *How do you feel about a road trip?*

I get back an old stand-by: Sun with a question mark drawn on her forehead in wine-colored lipstick.

Grabbing a sticky note and my trusty Sharpie, I draw an abbreviated family tree with a question mark in the spot where my father should be. Then I circle it in red and write "Ann Arbor" next to it.

My pulse is deafening as I wait for a response. It's entirely possible I'm nuts. Sun will tell me if I'm nuts.

It occurs to me that basing my own sanity on the judgment of a girl who once jumped off a garage into a swimming pool might not be the greatest plan I've ever had.

Her response chirps into my phone and fizzy relief

unwinds me until I'm slumped in my chair. All it says is:

When do we leave?

[17]

I DID A QUICK apology for storming out on my mom, and since she so prefers to avoid the topic of my biological father, she let it go. And let me borrow her car.

I don't know how I'm going to explain the mileage. That's the only thing I can't figure out. It's a problem, for sure, but not enough of one to stop me as Sun and I fly down the highway in my mother's Jeep Cherokee. Our cover story is a spontaneous trip to Great America. It's not a horrible cover – it'll explain why we're gone all day, but it's about 300 miles short of our actual destination. Not to mention the 300 extra miles on the way back. All I can do is hope she didn't know what was on the odometer before I left.

Sun is full of the manic cheer she always gets doing something bad. I'm...sweaty. I don't know if I'm more nervous about deceiving my parents or the possibility of seeing my biological father. Chad.

I still can't get over the name.

"Last chance to ride the rolly-coasters!" Sun chirps as we approach the Gurnee, Illinois exit. She makes a waving motion with her hand to indicate the tracks we can see rising into the air on our left.

"Not today." I signal and change to the left lane.

Sun rolls down her window, drowning out the stereo with whipping wind, and howls, "Yeah, bitches, road trip!" into the void. She grins at me when the window is back up, pieces of her pink hair clinging to the frames of her gold Elvis sunglasses.

"Re-watching *Breaking Bad* again?" I ask.

"Science, bitches!" she quotes.

I laugh, taking each hand off the wheel in turn to wipe my palms on my thighs. "Next stop, Ann Arbor."

OKAY, SO THE next stop is actually near the Indiana border when we're both dying for a bathroom break and something to drink. Close enough.

Sun does a few of her improvised yoga stretches in front of the vast drink cooler of the rest stop.

"What are you going to say to him?" she asks for the third time since we left.

I give the same answer I have the first two times. "I have no idea."

She straightens up. "We should rehearse it or something."

"That would be weird."

"If we don't, you're probably going to walk up to this guy, burst into tears and ask him where the bathroom is."

My stomach swoops like a bird avoiding a predator. She's so, so right. "Okay, okay. What do I say?"

She puffs out her chest and tries to look down at me like she's taller. When she speaks, her voice is deep and strangely cheerful. "Well, well, well, little girl, what can I do for you?"

"Oh my God, my father is not Santa Claus."

Putting her hands on her belly, she laughs. "Ho ho ho, Mariska, I'm your father."

"Now I'm going to have nightmares about Darth Vader in a Santa suit."

Sun laughs so hard she has to lean against the Gatorade cooler. "O.M.G., I feel a fanfic coming on!"

"You're not helping."

She laughs a while longer before she manages to say, "I'm sorry. You're right."

"What am I doing, Sun?"

Now the laughter is completely gone from her face. "You don't want to turn around, do you?"

My stomach churns and my heart seems to tug in opposite directions at the same time. "I don't know. Yes. No. I don't know." I chew the inside of my cheek.

"Tell you what. I'll buy you a frappucino and we'll drive a little further while you drink it. Then you decide."

I nod and let her lead me down the aisle to the bottled coffee drinks.

———

IN SAWYER, MICHIGAN, we stop for lunch, but I can't take more than a few bites.

"You wanna try again?" Sun asks.

I put down my sandwich and take a breath. "Hi. You don't know me, but I think you knew my mom once."

"Who's your mom?" Her tone is deeper than usual, but flat and nothing like the weird Santa voice she used earlier.

"Lauren Bokori," I say. "You guys met at Burning Man about eighteen years ago."

"And if he doesn't remember?" Sun prompts in her own voice.

I wipe my palms on my thighs again. "Well,

anyway, it turns out you're my father."

Her eyes go wide. "Whoa. Way to bury the lede!"

"Okay, forget it." I shake my head. "I can't do this."

"No no! I like it that way. That was way better than the last time." She nods encouragingly. "Do it that way."

I stare at her for a long time, running through possible reactions my father might have to the big news. But I can't possibly predict what he'll do. He could ignore me completely. He could call me a liar. He could throw his arms around me and hug me like a big reunion scene in a movie. He could curse me out.

"Why am I doing this?" I whisper.

"You don't have to," Sun reminds me.

"I know."

"Do you want to go home?"

"Let's just drive a little further and then decide."

———

THAT'S HOW IT goes all the way to Ann Arbor. We'll just drive a little further and then decide. And then it's too late to decide because we're already here. The GPS unit Sun borrowed from her dad leads us through the city until we can't go any further. Apparently no one informed the GPS satellites about the Street Art Fair.

"Now what?"

"Now we find a place to park. I gotta pee."

So I cruise for a bit and pull into a municipal lot not too far from the barricaded streets where white tents line the curb, each housing a different artist. We find a bank of port-a-potties and Sun dances from foot to foot until one opens up.

She darts inside, but peeks her head through the door to give me the usual warning. "Don't let anyone tip this thing over while I'm inside."

"Wouldn't dream of it." I cross my arms over my chest and try to decide for the millionth time if I'm crazy.

"Am I crazy?" I ask Sun when she emerges, making dramatic gagging gestures.

"God it stinks in there! Yes, of course you're crazy."

I feel my face take on the shape of pure panic. "What am I doing here? What the hell do I expect to get out of this?"

Sun grips my shoulders and nods sharply to make her glasses slide down enough to make eye contact. "Whatever you want to get."

"I don't know what I want."

She smiles. Not the manic, badness-inspired grin, but a soft, almost sad smile. "Who the hell does?"

I step forward and wrap my arms around her waist, resting my cheek on her shoulder. "I'm sorry I dragged you here."

She returns the hug with bone-crushing ferocity. "I don't accept."

Tears thicken the laugh that rides out what air she's left in my lungs.

"Now." Taking my shoulders again, she pushes me back to arm's length. "Are you seriously, *seriously* going to drive all the way to Michigan and back in one day without at least *looking* at the man who..." here she hesitates, "who unwittingly donated his sperm to your genetic code?"

I laugh. "That might be the most disgusting thing anyone has ever said about someone's father."

"Pssh. Not even close. Give me a second and I'll gross you out so bad you'll need years of therapy."

"Please don't."

She smiles that same sad smile, and uses her thumbs to wipe the tears off my cheeks. "Mariska, I am dead serious when I tell you I will turn around and go home right now, but I have to admit I am just about nuclear with curiosity. What do you want to do?"

Why can't anything be straight forward? Why can't it all be simple?

I stuff the phone back in my pocket and look into

Sun's eyes. "Let's find him."

THE MAP WE get from the official visitors' booth is kind of hard to follow at first with the booths all numbered on the map, but not on the actual tents. But after a bit of touristy gawking, we find the row.

His booth is about halfway down the row and as we approach, my feet stop cooperating. I walk slower and slower until I'm at a stop two booths away from The Limit. Yes, his sign still says The Limit.

Suddenly I am violently embarrassed for him. Presumably he is in his forties, and he's still going by that name. Is it because he's so successful he has to keep it? Or is he clinging to some image of himself that doesn't exist?

Sun doesn't notice I've stopped until she's almost at his booth. Her double-take is almost comical when she looks back for me, but I don't laugh. She hurries back to me.

"Can't do it?" she asks without judgment.

I shake my head. "I don't know if I want to."

Her magenta lips disappear into a flat press for a moment. "Should we walk a little further and then decide?" she asks.

I try to say no, but only the shape of the word makes it to my mouth. Sun takes my arm and guides me to the side of the path away from Chad "The Limit" Donoughue.

"It's your call," she says.

I throw my arms around her, eyes stinging. "You are literally the best friend in the history of ever."

She hugs me back. "I know."

"What am I going to do without you?"

Forcing me back, she grabs both sides of my face and forces me to look down into her eyes. "You will never ever be without me."

"Okay." I nod and she lets go of my head.

"Now, you are literally the closest you have ever been to your bio dad. Do you want to meet him?"

I think about it, but there's no answer in my head, so I cast about in the rest of my body. Heart, guts, nerves. Nobody seems to know what to do.

"Do you want me to check him out for you?" Her eyes flash. "I'm kind of dying to see the guy."

"Yes."

With a grin, Sun turns and starts down the path. She's only a few steps away when my feet make a decision and I dart after her. I crash into her, wrapping my arms around her waist. "I'm coming with you."

She presses her hands over mine. "Good."

We creep close enough to get a good look into the booth. There's a forty-something guy inside, tilted back on a folding chair. He's got darkish hair, cropped close to his head, and an oversized mustache. He's wearing a leather apron over a black t-shirt with the neck and sleeves cut off and a bandana hangs loose around his throat. All around him are metal hulks of various sizes.

"That's your dad," Sun whispers.

I stare at him for a long time without speaking. He's browsing a smart phone, totally unaware that his eighteen-year-old daughter is standing a dozen feet away from him.

Finally, I shake my head. "That's not my dad. My dad's name is Ray."

Sun squeezes my arms, still wrapped tightly around her from behind. "What do you want to do?"

And it comes to me. I let go of my best friend and swing my backpack around with a practiced gesture. Reaching inside, I pull out my camera and pop off the lens cap. I don't even care what the settings are. This isn't a portrait. I raise the viewfinder to my eye and fire off a snapshot. A quick glance at the LCD tells me it's good enough.

"I'm ready to go."

"You got it." She turns and takes me by the hand to tow me through the crowd, back the direction we came. At the end of the aisle, she pauses. "Are you sure?"

"Yes."

"This is your last chance."

I look toward The Limit. "That guy doesn't have anything to do with me. Let's go home."

[18]

SUN AND I alternate driving for the five-hour trip
home. It's nearly nine p.m. when we get back to
Milwaukee. We've been on the road all day, but I'm still
hyped up.

Just as we'd crossed the border into Wisconsin, I'd
gotten a text message from Blake. Finally!

Back in town. You around later?

I replied with a non-committal, *Maybe. What's up?*

My phone chirps with Blake's response. *Why don't
you come by? I'm in my new place on campus.* He follows
that with an address and my stomach flutters. I've been
alone with boys before, but always with the threat of
parents returning. This feels...weird. I haven't even seen
him in over a year and he's inviting me to his apartment? Is
that allowed with a sort-of, almost ex?

On the other hand, I feel like it would be easier to
explain what I want him to do in person.

"Are you seriously going to go?" Sun asks me as I

pull into her driveway.

"Yeah," I answer, proud of the calm in my voice. "What's the big deal?"

She squints at me. "Don't do anything stupid, okay?"

"Like drive ten hours to take a picture of a complete stranger?"

"Yeah, like that." She grins.

"I won't."

We hug over the console and she hops out. "Be safe," she calls before closing the door.

I roll the window down and call out, "I love you!"

"Love you too, girl."

I stab the power button on the radio for distraction as I head for Blake's apartment. Commercial, commercial, commercial, music. A song is just ending. The DJ comes on to do station identification, and tell us what's coming up before launching into the song that had been playing on Caine's iPod down in the dark room. My stomach clenches as memories washes over me.

Warm hands on my hips, warm lips against mine, the soft, swarming dark and the familiar tang of chemicals in the air...

I poke the power button again. Silence is a better choice just now.

THE DRIVE TO Blake's leaves my palms sweaty and my stomach in knots. I don't know why I'm so nervous to ask him to help me. We were even sort of friends in high school, making out notwithstanding. Why wouldn't he help me? What am I freaking out about?

After finding a parking space, I kill the engine and rest my head on the steering wheel. How am I supposed to know what to do in this situation? Who gets into this kind of situation? *Is* this a situation?

Deep breathing. That's a good first step. After a couple of those, I'm bound to feel better. Better-ish. Better-ish enough to get out of the car anyway.

The few people I pass on the sidewalk are clearly students. I feel very awkward and obvious as I check addresses all the way down the block. Everyone must know I'm younger than them. Even if there are other freshmen in the crowd, they've already moved into their dorms and apartments. I am still living at home, therefore I might as well be in junior high.

Blake's building looks promising. Smallish, with a clean foyer. There are no names on the brass mailboxes, but he told me he was in 2C, so I ring that bell. After a few tries, someone buzzes the security door and I yank it open in a panic. I'm always convinced I'll miss the window of opportunity with remote locks. I don't know why.

Inside, a murmuring mishmash of sounds come from all the surrounding apartments, making me feel like an invader. I try to walk on tiptoes to the stairs without looking like I'm actually walking on tiptoes.

Upstairs, the common areas are less promising. Thin, worn, industrial carpet with a frightening number of stains. The door to 2C is ajar, but I knock as I enter.

"Mariska Bokori! You found it!" Blake smiles at me, getting up from a tired-looking couch.

"Hi." My stomach flutters at the sight of him. Oh my, he is so very cute. How could I have forgotten? He's tall and athletic, with sandy brown hair that is nowhere near the length that officially looks shitty on guys. He's grinning, showing off his straight white teeth. He could be in a toothpaste commercial.

"Come on in!" He waves me into the living room, where two other guys are still sitting on the couch watching baseball. "Guys, this is Mariska. Mariska, my roommates. You wanna see our place?"

"Yeah, sure." I think of Caine the moment I say the words, realizing it's something he says a lot. My cheeks get hot, and I wish I could snatch the words out of the air and stuff them in my pocket, but of course Blake has no idea I'm quoting anyone.

Caine would be horrified to know I was quoting him with such a pedestrian phrase.

I have to stop thinking about Caine.

Blake leads me into the small kitchen, which strangely only features two cabinets. On a cart below the microwave, I spot a bulk box of Ramen noodles. Chicken flavor.

"You want a beer?" he asks, opening the 'fridge to reveal two cases of Milwaukee's Best and a bag of oranges. COLLEGE STUDENTS FIGHT SCURVY WHILE DRINKING, see Health.

"Sure." I don't, not really, but I am not going to be the lame high school girl who turns down a beer in a college guy's apartment. He opens the can for me and I take a demonstration sip. "Thanks."

"Come on, you gotta see my room."

The butterflies in my stomach have turned to a flock of gulls. If I drink this beer, I will definitely throw up. But I smile and follow him down the short hall to a bedroom with white walls and dingy off-white carpet. Why do rentals always have light carpet?

He's got the usual bedroom stuff: bed, desk, dresser, stereo equipment, and a TV that is way too big for the room. It's on the floor in the corner, with a snakes' nest of cables behind it. There are a few posters on the wall, that famous one from *Animal House* and one with rows and rows of beer bottles. Also a pennant for Marquette and a Green Bay Packers Fan Parking Only sign over the desk.

The whole thing looks distinctly lived in, and kind of cliché. As if he'd ordered up everything from a catalog called *College Guy Living*. The only unexpected piece is a poster of different fractals. Each one is no bigger than a postcard, but all together they make a quilt of colors and negative space. Even from across the room I can see the Mandelbrot set.

I point to it. "I didn't know you were into math."

"Huh?" He looks where I'm indicating.

"The fractals." I smile, in love with the idea that Blake Mitchell is a closet math nerd. "Very cool."

"Trippy right?" He laughs. "I like the colors."

I walk closer and point to one. "I used to know which polynomial this one was. Mrs. Reynolds – remember her? – she had a few of these in the room where we used to prep for Decathlon."

"You were in track? I never knew that." He grins.

"Academic Decathlon," I correct.

"Oh." His grin fades, but he nods. "What's a poly — what'd you say?"

"The fractals." I tap the poster again. "These are all different equations, but I only know one of them. Or, I used to anyway...." I trail off when I realize he has no idea what I'm talking about. Nerves lash around my throat. "Never mind."

Blake laughs. "Whatever you say, Pretty Girl."

I swallow and try not to think about my ears. Maybe if I pretend I don't even have ears, they won't turn red. I need to get out of this nerdy territory. *Pronto.* "So... how have you been? How was the cabin?"

"So great. We had a blast. He's got this new JetSki...." He whistles.

"Oh." I feel so, so awkward and stupid. Is this what college is like? I am going to be so awful at this.

"We got back on Sunday and I moved in here Monday. It's been crazy." He laughs, making me wonder what the joke might be, but it's one of those laughs you can't help joining.

"That sounds pretty crazy."

"But I told you I'd call you, didn't I?" He holds a hand out like maybe I'm supposed to shake it or give him a low five. I have no idea what to do so I sort of set my hand on his with moderate force. Either a weak five or a vigorous handshake. Either way, I'm sure I did it wrong. But he closes his fingers around mine before I can pull my stupid hand back.

"You did."

"Let's sit while you drink your beer." He doesn't let go of my hand as he backs toward the bed, and I find myself pulled along with him. There is a very distinct possibility I'm going to asphyxiate on my own pounding heart. "What have you been up to?"

I tell him everything. I don't mean to do it all in a rush like I do, but I'm nervous. I'm sick nervous. I'm feeling guilty and weird and out-of-place, and I can't shut myself up. So, I tell him about everything that's happened: packing up my room, the boxes, Ray. O'Neill's car, the Starlight drive-in being leveled, the twins, my mom's redecorating obsession, Sun, ninjas, bicycle cops, Pseudo Prom, the photographer at the lakefront...everything but Caine, and the road trip I just took with Sun. Guilt is a rotten fruit in my stomach.

He listens, nodding and laughing a few times, finishing his can of beer while I talk. Meanwhile, my beer stays untouched, only sweating in my hand and no doubt getting more bitter with every degree it warms. I don't care; I didn't want it anyway.

Finally, I just have to shut my mouth. There's nothing left to say that won't end in me gushing about how nervous I am.

"So were you in the paper?" he asks.

"I didn't see anything yet. I don't know if it'll happen."

"But there are pictures of the ninja thing on-line already, huh?"

"Yeah. I haven't checked yet today, but there were already showing up the day we did it."

He laughs. "That's awesome!"

I feel considerably less dorky now that he said that.

"We should check." He grabs a laptop off the desk and drops onto the bed, just a little closer to me than he was before. He goes online and does a quick search for *ninjas flying kites*. Twenty or so pictures come up from different users. Plus it gives him a handful of links, including the same Instagram listings, but also a few blogs, two Twitter mentions, and a YouTube video.

"Look at you, you're famous!" He bumps me with his shoulder.

Blushing, I squirm in my seat. "It was kind of Sun's big idea."

"Who cares whose idea it was?" He clicks on the video. It's terrible quality, and the sound is nothing but rushing wind, but it's clearly us. Ten ninjas.

"So who was all there?" he asks.

I try to point everyone out, but it's hard when the

video is mostly black blobs.

"You know, if you did something like this here at Marquette, you probably would have gotten a hundred ninjas out there. This is truly hilarious." He laughs.

I smile, but my gut reaction is No. I wouldn't have wanted a bunch of strangers involved. This was my little moment of strangeness. A secret – if almost a dozen people can be said to keep a secret. "It worked out okay."

"You really are something, Mariska Bokori."

The butterflies in my stomach are ready to combust. "I'm not sure if that's a compliment or not."

"It's a compliment." He closes the lid of his computer – there's a big M sticker on the lid – and leans down to set it on the floor. Then he takes my beer from me and sets it on the floor as well. Too close to the computer for my comfort, but I guess that's not my problem.

Blake smiles at me and cups my cheek. "You're adorable, do you know that?" Before I can answer, he kisses me. It's wet, and hard, and I don't want it.

I lean back. "Don't."

He pulls away and smiles at me. "What's wrong?"

I shake my head, biting my lip. "I wanted to ask you something." But do I? I feel gross being here with him. He's not what I remembered. We haven't even seen each other in a year and he's trying to suck my face off within ten minutes?

He laughs. "My bad." He laughs so easily. I don't have to do anything to earn it. "What's up?"

A bundle of nerves jumps in my stomach. I can't decide how I feel about the words I know are about to come out of my mouth. "Do you want to come to my prom thing?"

"Me?"

"Yeah, sure." Caine's phrase again. Damn it. It's like I'm living in the *Tell-Tale Heart* of kissing.

He laughs. "We already did prom."

"I know." I sit up. "But I lost my picture, so...I'm doing it again."

"I'm not even sure where my picture is."

"I guess I'm kind of sentimental."

"Don't worry, Pretty Girl. I think it's cute."

Okay, so he laughs a lot and he has bad taste in room decor. But, he calls me Pretty Girl and he looks at me like I'm fascinating. I smile at him, the nerves in my stomach finally settling. "So...you wanna come with me? Go back in time for a night?"

He laughs again. "I'm sure it's gonna be really cute, but it's kind of my first weekend back on campus so...." He shrugs. "There's some parties and stuff."

"Oh. Right." That's another picture I'll never get

back.

"But, hey...we're here right now, aren't we?"

I nod, but I don't really mean it.

"I'm glad you came down here. You're even cuter than I remember." He leans into me but I scoot backwards, then stand up.

"No." I shake my head, feeling a weird smile yank at my mouth. "Can I ask you something else?"

He grins. "Shoot."

"Why did you take me to prom in high school?"

He laughs. Of course. Then he stretches out on the bed and looks at me in a lazy way I think he intends to be sexy. "You're cute." He shrugs. "And you were, like, no pressure. Nobody was going to make a big deal out of it if I took you, like they would have if I took Kayleigh." His ex-girlfriend.

I press my hand into my stomach. Partly because I feel like I'm going to throw up. And partly because it gives me something to do with my hands rather than snatching his Chemistry textbook off his desk to throw at him. My nose is burning, but for the first time in two weeks, it's not because of sadness. The only tears waiting for me now are angry ones.

"I think...I think I'm just gonna go."

"Did I do something wrong?" he asks with such

honest surprise I wonder how he got into college at all.

I smile, but it's not at him. And it's not a happy smile by any means. "Wow. I just made us up in my head, didn't I?"

"Huh?"

"Never mind." I wave at him. "I'm just gonna go. Thanks."

"What the hell, Mariska?" he says.

"I know. This probably seems crazy to you, but just think, you're better off without the crazy girl, right?"

I smile at him with a final wave and let myself out of the apartment. His roommates don't even look up from the ballgame.

I don't stop until I get back to the sidewalk, then I pause to take a picture of myself in front of the address plate on the wall next to the door. I make a gagging face with one finger pointing into my open mouth and send it to Sun with the caption, *Blake Mitchell sucks*.

Right away I get back, *What did he do to you? I'll kill him!*

Nothing, promise. Just wasted my time.

Wanna talk?

I'm fine. No worries. I have something I have to do tonight.

[19]

MY PARENTS ARE still up watching Comedy Central
when I get home. I'm glad they're still up, but at the same
time, that means I have to go through with the first part of
the plan I formulated on the way home, and that doesn't
sound quite so pleasant.

"Hey Mara, how was Six Flags?" Ray asks when I
come in.

I don't answer right away, walking all the way into
the living room to stand near the TV. My mom
immediately looks concerned and mutes the TV.

"Are you okay, sweetie?" she asks.

"I have to tell you guys something."

Ray goes tense. "Is the car okay?"

"The car's fine." I hold up both hands. "I just...."
And now I can't figure out where to start. We didn't go to
Six Flags? We sort of drove to Michigan today? I've
actually been back for a few hours but I went to this college
guy's apartment?

It's been a hell of a day.

I pull out my camera and bring up the picture I snapped in Ann Arbor. I hand it over to my mom first, who looks bewildered.

"What's this?"

I swallow hard. "The Limit."

She still looks utterly lost for a long moment, then suddenly sits bolt upright. "What?"

"I found him online, and he was at this art festival and I…I lost the only picture I had, so I…Sun and I…."

My mother's face is ashen. "What did you do?"

"Nothing." I shake my head quickly. "He never even saw me. I just took this picture and we left."

"Why?" she asks at the same time Ray asks, "Where was this?"

I decide to skirt Ray's question for now. Maybe they can live without knowing I've been through four states today. "I thought it was something I could get back. But it wasn't like that at all. It was—" I break off. "I can't explain."

"I cannot believe you would do this!" My mom shoves the camera at Ray, and I try not to wince at her rough handling of my baby. "Without telling me? Why would you even want to…what does he have to do with…I can't believe this!"

"I'm sorry." I really am. I feel bad that I deceived them. "I knew you'd never want me to go."

"Not by yourself. Do you know how dangerous that was? Did you think you were just going to waltz up to a complete stranger and introduce yourself? Do you really think he would have just been happy to meet you?"

Ouch. "What was I supposed to do, ask you to come along? You don't care anything about him. You don't even know his real name. It's Chad, by the way."

"Chad?" Ray can't help interrupting, and he looks as startled by the name as I was.

Mom glares at him, and he quickly looks down at the camera.

"No, I don't care anything about him. Why should I? I doubt he knew my name! It wasn't about that."

Ugh, I really hate being reminded that my mother had a one-night stand with a stranger while tripping on mushrooms. It's bad enough knowing it happened, but when she talks about it, I can't help getting visuals.

"See? I knew you wouldn't want me to go."

"Of course I wouldn't want you to, but if it was that important to you, we could have worked something out."

"Seriously, Mom? You'd rather forget it ever happened."

"That is not true."

"Yes it is. You don't want anything to do with your past. You're always throwing it away. But I'm not like you."

"All right, that's enough of this. Come with me." She's off the couch before I even know she's moving. She strides to the hall with all the snap of a drill sergeant.

"What?"

"Come with me." She flicks her fingers toward her palms. "Now."

I do what she says, following me to her bedroom. She leaves me standing in the center of the room and goes into the walk-in closet. I can't see what she's doing, but I can hear muffled sounds and her strained breath. Then, she emerges with a small teal document box. She holds it out to me.

"Open it."

I walk to the bed and set the box on it to remove the lid. Inside, I find a collection of things from my childhood. A copy of every school picture, a penmanship award from fourth grade, my report cards, the small felt pouch in the shape of a tooth where I used to leave my baby teeth for the tooth fairy. A tiny jar full of those baby teeth. An ID band from the hospital, too tiny to be anything but the one I got when I was born. A hand-drawn Mother's Day card. More things I can't immediately identify.

"Happy now?" she asks.

"You kept all this stuff?" My eyes are back to not-blinking. I had no idea.

"Of course I kept all this stuff! You're my daughter. My baby."

Part of me bristles at being called her baby, but another part of me wants to walk into her arms and be just that. "But I thought...."

"Just because I don't have every piece of paper you've ever touched doesn't mean it didn't matter to me." She props one fist on her hip. "I would have had to build an addition to the house to keep everything you ever did."

"But...." I swallow around a lump in my throat. "All the big clean outs. All my toys and books...."

"Were you using them?" she asks with a raised eyebrow.

"No."

"There are things that matter to me and things that don't. You matter. You made the cut. A bunch of Bratz dolls don't. And neither did the guy who just happened to unwittingly donate sperm to me one night."

"Oh."

"Yeah. Oh." Her hand comes loose from her hip and she puts that arm around my shoulders. "Now can you stop sniping at me?"

"I'm sorry."

"Well, I did ask you to go easy on Ray. I guess I should have realized you'd go hard on me instead."

Now I feel about three inches tall. "I'm really sorry."

"Good." She pats my back. "And I'm sorry your box is gone."

"I guess I get my box habit from you." I nod at the open one on her bed.

"You just need to work on scale." She pinches two fingers together to show I need to cut back. "Figure out what actually matters."

"Yeah, yeah."

"Hey, look at it this way – at least you get to learn your lesson this way instead of ending up pregnant at Burning Man."

"Ew."

"Hey, I got you out of the bargain. I'm pretty satisfied."

And she's being so nice. So nice when she has every right to be furious, that I am undone. I let loose with a choking wail and throw my arms around her.

"I'm sorry, Mom. I shouldn't have lied to you."

She hugs me for a long time before she says, "No you shouldn't have."

"It was stupid. I don't even know why I wanted to see him. He's not my dad. Ray is."

She eases me back and smiles at me with tears on her cheeks. "I think you just made someone's night." She nods over my shoulder and I turn to see Ray standing on the threshold of the bedroom. He's still holding my camera in one hand.

"We okay in here?" he asks.

I nod and cross the room to give him a hug. "I'm sorry."

"Um, sure, Mara." He seems a little confused.

Taking the camera from him, I select the picture of The Limit. I zoom in on his face for just a second, while Mom and Ray peek over my shoulder.

"Nice mustache," my mom mutters.

We all study the image silently for a moment, then I click the menu key and select Delete Image.

"Are you sure?" Ray asks.

"Yeah." I nod. "It's a lousy picture anyway."

And I've got other, better things to do with the rest of my night than stare at some stranger.

[20]

WHEN I GO back to school to pick up my pictures on Thursday, I look for Caine's car, but it's not there. I've got the newly embellished yearbook with me just in case, but I didn't really expect him to be here. Doesn't make me any less disappointed, though.

Mr. O'Neill is there, of course, and he leans back in his chair, fingers locked at the base of his skull in his familiar way when I take the keys back to him.

"Which pictures did you take?" he asks.

I delicately spread them out before him. Six 8x10 prints making up the sum total of my career as a newspaper photographer. O'Neill surveys the lot and taps his finger just below the picture of Valerie Gibb.

"I remember this one. You've got a knack, Bokori."

"Thanks."

"You found a yearbook, too, hmm?" He nods at the book in my arms.

"Sort of. This is actually Caine's. I've got to get it back to him."

"Looks like someone dropped it in a pool along the way."

The covers are no longer parallel. In all our back-

and-forthing, we'd already added enough to the pages to wear it in, but my project from last night really sealed its fate. The poor thing won't shut for anything anymore. "I made a few...adjustments."

He cocks an eyebrow. "Part of your reclamation project?"

"Sort of. It's kind of an argument we're having."

"Do I want to know?"

"It's about memories and keeping things from the past and whether or not you can remember the truth...I don't know exactly how to explain it."

He nods. "I understand. Nostalgia is a powerful thing. It can make you long for things you didn't even like that much the first time around."

I laugh softly, thinking of Blake. "That's true."

"But then again, without memory...." He shakes his head. "Greater men than me have said it better than I could. 'Those who cannot remember the past are condemned to repeat it,' just for starters."

"George Santayana." The name comes to me instantly, without thought, and I know it must have been an Academic Decathlon question once upon a time.

"Nice one. How about this? 'God gave us memory that we might have roses in December.'"

I shake my head.

"J.M. Barrie," he supplies.

"*Peter Pan.*"

He smiles. "Very good indeed."

"So what you're saying is that you're firmly undecided on the issue?" I ask.

"I'm certain it's not healthy to live for the past alone or the future alone." He raps once on the desktop. "The here and now is highly underrated, considering it's all we have access to."

I squeeze the yearbook to my chest. "Everything in moderation, and all that?"

He nods. "I think it's fair to say we did a sufficient job educating you, Bokori."

"I guess so."

"Now, if I'm not mistaken, you are a young lady with somewhere to be, and I am certainly an old man with too much work to do, so...." He flicks his hand at me.

I give him his moment of gruffness, collecting my prints and laying them carefully inside the front cover of the yearbook. The cartoon frog on the giant adhesive bookplate Caine applied greets me enthusiastically: *Please Return This Book To Mariska!* My name is written in large, careful block letters with a fat-tipped marker. I'd added a proofreader's caret and the word *DON'T* between *Please* and *Return* in large red letters.

"Thanks, Mr. O'Neill."

He looks up from his papers and gives me a genuine smile. "My pleasure."

I DO A DRIVE-BY of Caine's house, but his car is parked at the curb. I could attempt another porch drop for the yearbooks, but I don't want him to catch me sneaking away from the house. Nope, I've gone to this much trouble; I can go to the added trouble of mailing the thing.

If it'll fit in a box.

The book gapes at me from the passenger seat, and no matter how many times I push down on the cover, it stays ajar. It's kind of like it's smiling, I decide, and I smile back at it.

"You gonna stay with him this time?" I ask it.

It doesn't answer, but the pages still look happy, so I pat it again.

Even if Caine doesn't keep the book, I'm okay with it. Making all the changes to it that I did was cathartic. It was a funeral for my high school life, in a way. It's not over quite yet, but I'm less terrified for what comes next.

After all, it was in high school that I convinced myself Blake saw me as anything but a convenience. I can't believe I wasted any time and energy on him. I can't believe I thought there was anything between us. I can't believe I ever wanted him involved in this project at all. That guy laughs too damn much. He's like a human hyena. And he doesn't even know he has math equations on his wall.

O'Neill was right about nostalgia. Blake sure looked better in the rearview mirror.

———

FOR THE RECORD, it's really, really expensive to send four yearbooks through the mail. Not as expensive as it is to buy four brand new ones from the robber barons who print the damn things, but expensive.

———

TOTALLY WORTH IT.

[21]

I THINK I'M more excited about Pseudo Prom than I was about actual prom. Junior year I'd gone as Blake's date, while my senior year I went in a group of loosely assembled friends. I'd lost both of my professional pictures, but thanks to being in a group for my senior year, it'd been easy to get a copy of that one.

The picture is brilliant: everyone crammed in front of the backdrop. There were eight of us, and the picture is little more than a crush of faces. But it's nicely lit, and no one has red-eye. More than that, though, I love the flushed look of our cheeks and the way most of Ruthie's hair had fallen out of her fancy prom up-do, and the fact that Jeremy was wearing sunglasses, and Tim was wearing RaeAnn's corsage in his hair, and everyone was so clearly enjoying themselves.

I had thought the purpose of this evening was to recreate that moment with Blake, back when I thought it was the coolest thing in the world to be taken by a senior.

Turns out, I'd rather not remember that night at all.

What an idiot I turned out to be.

But at least I figured out that this night is about now. It's about *this* night, and these friends who have done so much for me in the last two weeks. I haven't yet managed to recreate any of the photos I've lost, but I've definitely connected with some of the feelings I felt during those lost moments. They're all layered together now. The old memories entangled with the act of recreating them. My own form of time-travel. Because now, when I look at Sun in her *hanbok*, I see my best friend at eighteen, but also at fourteen. Virginia Beach lurks in the weed-clotted skating pond at the park. Ninjas make me think of clowns, and the years of working for the paper are compressed into a happy blur of climbing into O'Neill's car.

So tonight, we are time travelers. Back to a past when we went to our beach-themed prom at the Riv, forward to a future where that night will be inextricably tied to this night – our present.

We have a pact, all of us who are part of this, that no one can spend more than twenty dollars on the night. So, when a horn honks in my driveway, it's not a limo, but Anna in her Mom's minivan. The rear doors slide open, and Sun and Cori jump out in their prom gear.

"I am so happy to have a reason to wear this

again." Sun pats her tiny white top hat with an affectionate, gloved hand. Behind the short veil of white netting, she's got her eyes made up with glitter and even a tiny rhinestone at the peak of her eyeliner. Her dress is real vintage. A 1950s tulle monstrosity in pale yellow that Sun actually screamed over when she found it in her grandmother's attic.

"You guys look great!" I can't help pressing one hand to my chest as happy tears threaten to make short work of my make-up.

"So do you." Sun winks at me from behind her veil.

"This might be the best idea you've ever had," Cori says, smoothing her hands over her totally-not-vintage purple dress. "Who gets to wear their prom dress twice?"

"Come on!" Anna gives the horn a little toot-toot! and waves us into the van. "We're gonna be late!"

I'M SHOCKED BY the number of prom goers when we get to the pizza place Sun and I chose for the occasion. It seemed like a good fit for a big group on a tight budget in formalwear. Now I'm just grateful the place features really long tables, because there are at least thirty people hanging around outside the entrance when Anna rolls into the parking lot.

"Holy crap," I breathe, whipping my head around as Anna cruises past the group. "Did you see that?"

Sun and Cori just laugh.

When I scramble out of the minivan, a male voice bellows, "Prom night, part two, baby!" and I can't help laughing. Even though this entire night has been my plan from the beginning, I feel like I just walked into my own surprise party.

I float on welcome hugs and enthusiasm as we enter the restaurant. Someone gives me a corsage – obviously homemade and probably from someone's garden at that – and I love it. All the girls have them. The other people in the restaurant look confused by us. I'm not surprised; it's August, after all, and this is a family pizza restaurant with a huge pipe organ for entertainment.

Conversation is impossible to keep track of while we eat off the huge silver trays balanced on the oversized cans of tomato sauce that serve at centerpieces in this place. I feel as fizzy as my soda, and my cheeks already hurt from smiling. I can't even see everyone at the table at once, so I find myself constantly leaning forward to peer down at the group. Sun has to stop me from leaning right into my pizza at least four times. I'm not sure I'd care if I did end up with a big, greasy, tomatoey stain on my chocolate brown dress, to be honest. It would somehow work for Pseudo Prom.

Across from me, Tim puts his arm around Ruthie and she leans into him with a grin. Laughing, she wipes a spot from the corner of his mouth with her napkin and he kisses her. I'm happy they get a second chance at prom – they weren't together the first time around. On the heels of that thought, I realize again how happy I am Blake isn't here.

What was I thinking?

My eyes have wandered during my reverie and I realize I'm staring at Mick.

"You know you didn't have to stage an entire second prom if you wanted to be my date," he says with a wink.

"What can I say? I'm a sucker for the big gesture."

"And nothing says, 'I secretly love you,' like pizza and pipe organ music, eh?" he says.

I just smile again and continue my visual survey of the table. Everyone seems to be having a good time. Everywhere I look, I see smiling faces and animated conversations. The pizza is disappearing and our harried waitress can't keep up with the refills on our pitchers of soda.

"Well," I say to Sun, "even if the Blue Canary is a

disaster, we've had the world's fanciest pizza party."

She laughs, making the ostrich plumes on her hat shiver and dance. "It's not going to be a disaster. It's going to be legendary!"

"All right, who's the birthday girl?" Our waitress is back, this time with an ice cream sundae in her hands. A single candle flickers on top.

Every hand at the table points at me.

"What?" Spontaneous cheek combustion. I look around in confusion.

Under the table, Sun pinches my thigh. "Go with it," she says through her teeth.

But she doesn't have to worry about me protesting, because the waitress is already setting the sundae in front of me.

"We've got a birthday!" The pipe organ player says into the microphone. "What's the name?"

Now my ears are on fire too. All up and down the table, I see nothing but grins.

Someone must give my name to the player, because the pipe organ blares to life on the familiar birthday tune and then the whole restaurant is singing to me. After the applause and cheers die down and the waitress is gone, I lean into the table again and demand to know what that was about.

"We knew you lost all your birthday cards and stuff too," Ruthie says, searching on her lap for something. I can only assume she's got a bag out of sight.

"So we figured we'd throw you a make-up birthday party as long as we were all here," Anna adds, holding out a sealed envelope with my name on it.

"Happy birthday, Mariska!" Cori jumps to her feet to stretch across the table and give me another envelope.

"Um...thanks." I barely have time to smile at her before someone is tapping me on the shoulder with another card. Envelopes come at me from every direction until I have a stack so thick I can't hold it with just one hand.

"You guys...." My vision blurs as I try to make eye contact with each person, and I have to stop to stare up into the lights, blinking rapidly. I don't want to break down at the table.

"Awww." Sun puts her arm around my shoulders and leans into me, getting her feathers in my face, but I don't care. I wrest my chair free from the crowded table and go up and down the line, giving everyone hugs and thank yous. This is the warmest and fuzziest I have ever felt. I can barely get the words out to thank everyone.

"God, you're a sap." Sun rolls her eyes when I get back to my chair.

"Thanks."

"Just promise you won't open them now, or we'll never be able to turn off the waterworks."

I nod.

"We should get a move on anyway," she says, rising from her seat. "Who's ready for some dancing?"

That would be everyone.

THE BLUE CANARY looks like a large, square robin's egg with a parking lot. It's a cinderblock number that more resembles a pale blue bunker than a dancehall, but the lighted sign announces *Fine Dining, Cocktails, Dancing*, and we can hear music when Jeremy pulls the door open.

Nerves clog my throat as we queue up. This is going to be a disaster, I am suddenly certain. But then my friends start disappearing into the building, and the line moves forward.

"You ready?" Sun asks, squeezing my elbow where her gloved hand rests in the crook.

"Yeah, sure." The words give me a stinging feeling in my diaphragm. I haven't heard from Caine since I mailed off my package. Days. I knew better than to think he'd come tonight.

Inside, the Blue Canary is an old-fashioned supper

club with high-backed leather booths arranged along the mirrored wall, a wooden bar, and a small orchestra set up in the northeast corner. The orchestra is playing one of those old songs I recognize but don't know the name of. Already, couples are circling the dance floor. Older couples – my grandparents' ages, and maybe older too. Some are keeping time in one spot, while others have got serious moves.

"Oh my God, I'm in love!" Sun squeals.

Once again, we're attracting a lot of attention, but the patrons of the Blue Canary look positively delighted to see the large group of young people. But from the look on the face of the man striding toward us, the feeling is not universal.

"Excuse me. Excuse me, can I help you?" He's wearing a black vest, a bow tie, a mustache, and a very sour expression.

Unseen hands shove me forward, and I realize I'm supposed to take point on this. "I'm sure this is going to sound crazy to you, sir, but I swear we're just here to dance."

"You know this isn't a nightclub," he says.

Sun snorts softly, but he doesn't seem to notice.

"We know." I nod seriously. "We'll be good, I swear."

He narrows his eyes, but says, "I don't want any trouble."

I blurt out, "It's my birthday!"

Beside me, Sun presses her white-gloved fingertips against her upper lip.

The bow tie guy says, "Happy birthday," in a way that somehow says the opposite. "I'll be keeping an eye on you kids."

Sun snorts and I kick her in the ankle, giving Mr. Mustache my best angelic smile.

"Thank you, sir."

"All right, let's dance!" Sun throws her arms in the air and I suddenly feel like I'm in a movie. And I want to dance.

[22]

I LEARN THE fox trot from an adorable old man named Roderick, cha-cha with a slightly less adorable old man named Simon, and waltz with the funniest little old man I've ever met, named Morris. I also dance with Tim, Jeremy, Mick, Sun, Anna, Ruthie and Justin. None of my friends are as skilled on the dance floor as any of the older regulars, but I really like the formal partner dancing. It's so much more romantic than the hug-and-sway I'm used to.

Not that I'm having romantic thoughts about Morris. Or any of them, for that matter. It's just the secret princess in me. I can't help it.

Sun is a hit with the little old ladies at the Canary. They can't stop exclaiming over her dress. One of them swears it used to be hers. Sun explains it was her grandmother's and the woman, Delores, says Sun wears it better than she ever did.

Taking a break at one of the leather banquettes, I

let my camera be my eyes for a bit, making the busy dance floor into a smear of colors and movement. There's no disco ball in this place, but the orchestra projects different colored lights on the dance floor, making my screen glow red, blue, white, green, and purple.

So my eyes can't quite believe what they're seeing when a certain familiar head of curly hair near the entrance shows up in the center of my lens. I push to my feet and weave through the spinning dancers to reach the door. I squint as I go, sure I'm not seeing what I think I'm seeing.

"Caine?"

He looks pale under the blue light currently bathing the room, but he gives me the ghostly smile. "Hi."

"What are you...?" I have a sudden urge to give my strapless dress a yank into alignment and check my hair. "I didn't...I didn't think you were coming."

"You asked me to." His expression doesn't change, but his eyes widen slightly.

"I know, but I thought...." I press my lips shut. "Did you get my package?"

The ghost of a smile returns. "Yeah."

My fidgeting hands accidentally set off the shutter on the camera around my neck lighting us up in the shock of the flash. I jump and Caine winces, slipping his thumb and ring finger beneath his glasses to rub at his eyes.

"Sorry." I force my hands to my sides where they grab hidden handfuls of my skirt.

"So...how's your second prom going?"

"Good." I twist, looking back at the dance floor for a moment. "I think I'm running off with an eighty-year-old man named Morris later."

"Which one is he?" Caine asks, stepping up beside me.

I watch for a sign of the charming, stooped little man with the fluffy white hair, and finally spot him dancing with a girl named Laura. "It appears he's keeping his options open." I point to Laura.

"Probably just letting her down easy." Caine's voice is close enough to make my right shoulder break into goose bumps.

"That would be his way."

We watch the dancers without talking until the end of the song. The band leader thanks the crowd for their polite applause then counts into the next song. I don't recognize it, or the dance moves that go along with it, but my fellow Pseudo Prom goers are gamely faking it in the counter-clockwise circle that defines the perimeter of the dance floor.

"I have something for you," Caine says, pulling my attention back to him.

"What?"

"Here." He pulls a messenger bag into view and produces the flared, abused yearbook I'd mailed to him on Wednesday. My heart drops like a stone into my stomach.

"Caine, I don't want it. I want you to have it."

"But I know how much it means to you." He holds it out.

"No." I shake my head. "Not anymore. You can do whatever you want with it." With one hand, I give the book a push in his direction.

"You're bluffing." He holds the book against his chest with crossed arms.

"No, I'm not. It's yours."

"What if I said I was going to throw it out?"

I study his face. He may have his usual neutral look, but I think I'm finally starting to decode the fine variations in the way he holds himself, and the things he thinks he keeps hidden in his eyes. He's the one bluffing. "Go ahead."

He studies me with curiosity. "You really mean it, don't you?"

"Yes. And I think it's good for me not to have this." I tap the book, still in his hands. "Besides, it's a little insulting to return a gift, don't you think?"

"A gift?" His eyebrows could be a still life called

Disbelief.

"I put a lot of work into that thing!"

His spectral smile returns. "I'll keep it on one condition."

"What's that?"

"You gotta fix this page." He cracks the binding, and even over the music I can hear the crinkle and creak of the pages – they're pretty overloaded with glue. Wonder if I should have used tape? Caine's fingers pry apart a few of the more pugnacious pages.

There's the spot where I glued in the picture of him flying my rainbow kite, right over the freshman girls' volleyball team.

There's the one from last week, with everyone jammed into O'Neill's car like sardines. It's pasted over the action shots of the JV swim team.

There, over the German club, I pasted in an index card where I'd written out the recipe for peanut butter Rice Krispie treats.

There's the place where I smoothed over the junior student council with a copy of the score card from Academic Decathlon, which I scanned in and shrunk down to half size.

There, a wide green maple leaf from the treehouse tree, ironed between two sheets of wax paper and glued over the first page of the freshman class collage.

It's no wonder the thing can't close.

Finally, he finds what he's looking for. The prom layout. It's mostly candids, save the posed picture of the King (Ammar Vasavada) and Queen (Tisha Bellcanto) in front of the beach backdrop. I've always hated the picture. It's poorly composed with too much empty space above their heads and slightly grainy for some reason. I can't imagine why the professional photographer would have even included this one in the package for the yearbook staff to choose from.

"I need a better picture than this one." He taps his finger on Ammar's face. "He hated Tisha. He won't mind if we cover this up."

"What do you want to put there?" I ask.

"I want a picture of the Pseudo Prom Queen." He looks at me.

"Me?"

"Who else would be the Queen of this thing?"

My cheeks flame, but the stage lights have gone red, so I hope it doesn't show. "If I do that, you'll keep it?"

He nods. "Promise."

"Okay. Deal." I hold out my hand and he shakes it solemnly.

"Holy crap, is that Caine?" Sun's voice arrives long

before the rest of her. "Look at you, Citizen! You clean up nice."

For some reason that makes me blush harder. Bless the inventor of the multicolored LED light.

She's right though, he looks...good. No cargo shorts with fraying pockets, no Nagano Winter Olympics t-shirt, no earphones. Instead, he's wearing a white button-down shirt with a tie, under a charcoal gray vest, and dress pants. I can hardly believe he even owns clothes like this, much less that he'd put them on to come to Pseudo Prom.

"So, do you dance or what?" Sun asks, jerking her thumb at the dance floor.

"Not – not really so much...no. Um, not at all."

She rolls her eyes, but I laugh.

"Pathetic. I'm taking this girl for a spin, okay?" Sun takes my hand and pulls me onto the dance floor, where everyone seems to be doing an easy swing step. I learned this one in gym class, back in junior high, so it's easy enough to settle into the rhythm and let Sun occasionally twirl me under her arm.

We pass Morris, who growls, "Lookin' good, girls!"

"This is way better than actual prom was," Sun says.

"Agreed." We circle the floor with the flow of

dancing traffic, and I do my best to keep Caine in view, but it's not always possible.

"Why are you rubber-necking?" Sun does an imitation of me, darting her head around like a woodpecker.

"I'm just making sure Caine's not bored out of his mind."

"Relax. He's a big boy, I'm sure he can take care of himself." She twirls me under her arm, and my camera thwacks her in the ribs as we come back together. "Oof."

"Sorry." I can't see over Sun's ostrich plumes. "It's just...I didn't think he was going to come."

"Oh my God." She stops dancing suddenly and I bump into her. A second later, another couple bumps into us, so Sun hauls me by the elbow to a corner of the dance floor where we won't obstruct the flow. "You like him, don't you?"

"What? No, I...." I look down at my camera. "I just...it's just...we've just been hanging out a lot, I guess, and I just...." I should tell her he kissed me, but I don't.

"Yeah, yeah, yeah." She waves her hand, impatient. "You just like him."

I raise my camera and fire off the flash in her face.

She rears back and pinches the bridge of her nose with her fingers. "Ah, God! That was uncalled for!"

"Accident."

"Liar." She props her fists on her hips and fixes me with a studying glare. "And your brattiness only proves it. You. Like. Caine."

"I wouldn't call it *that,* necessarily." I roll my eyes.

"Oh my stars." She fans herself. "You are ridiculous. I have to get away from your ridiculousness before I start to get soft in the head."

"Sun, shut up."

She grins at me, making the rhinestones in the corners of her eyes glint. "Adorable. Hilarious, but adorable. Hidorable, if you will."

"Okay, for real shut up."

She mimics zipping her lips, then locking them and throwing away the key. An X crossed over her heart is the final touch before she puts one hand on my back and gives me a shove toward the booth where we last saw Caine.

He's not there anymore, and right away my heart starts hammering. I wheel around, looking for the exit, but I don't see his dark spiral curls anywhere among the white hairs. Spinning again, I scan the whole place until I spot him sitting on the edge of another booth with Ruthie and Tim. Talking. Just talking.

I press a hand over my heart and force a deep breath. I am ridiculous. It will be better for everyone if I find myself a distraction. Luckily, I happen to be in a dance hall and it doesn't take long to find a willing partner. I make it through three songs before my legs feel like jelly and I'm starting to sweat more than I like. Thanking my last partner, I excuse myself to the semi-circle booth where a lot of my friends are gathered – Caine included.

"I have a surprise!" Myra announces when I get close enough. She doesn't wait for a response before producing a pair of cheap plastic crowns. "Look! For the King and Queen."

"There's a King and Queen?" Ruthie demands, leaning in for a better look at the ridiculous crowns. They're gold with large, fake jewels at the peaks. In the back, there is a snap closure that can be adjusted for different sizes. Ruthie bursts out laughing.

I have to agree, they're hilarious. Not the silvery, rhinestoned confections from actual prom. "Perfect," I tell Myra.

"But who's the King and Queen?" Ruthie wants to know.

Myra looks at her like she's nuts. "Um, all of us. Are you kidding me?" She sets one of the crowns on her own head and reaches out to put the other on Miguel's head. "Ta-da! We're royalty!"

"Take our picture!" Miguel puts his arm around

Myra's shoulders and gives me a kajillion-watt grin. I take a quick picture of them, but they're sitting down and my flash bounces off the mirror behind them. I scowl at the display screen.

"We're gonna need to find a better place for portraits," I tell them.

"Well, then let's go!" Miguel stands on the seat of the booth and picks his way past everyone blocking his way.

I'm glad to have him with me as we go in search of a better portrait spot. He's the one who recommended this place, and I know he's been here with his dance troupe before. Near the back, in the hallway by the bathrooms, we find the ideal location. It's a mural of a starlit night with a full moon. In the foreground, there is a large stylized tree with a single bird sitting on a branch. A trail of music notes flows from the bird's beak. It's tight quarters, with the opposite wall being so close, but I find I can get a decent shot of Miguel as long as I stand inside just the ladies' room and prop the door with my foot. The light from the bathroom helps, too.

For over an hour, I stand like that, pausing only when patrons come back to use the ladies' room. My friends come back in pairs, in groups, and a few come alone for their chance to wear the silly plastic crown and get their picture taken. I only give up the camera twice, each time to Mick, who will be taking over as staff photographer for the paper in a matter of days. The first time I give it up to get in a group picture with all the people I went to actual Prom with. The second time I give it up is for Caine.

"You promised," is all he says, pointing at the mural with one hand and reaching for my camera with the other.

"By myself?" I ask.

"You promised."

"At least let me get Mick."

"If you insist."

Mick takes the picture for me, but then he insists that Caine join me against the backdrop. "Come on," Mick says. "Mariska will be pissed if she has a picture of everyone but you."

I blush, even though he didn't mean that the way my cheeks are taking it.

Caine agrees without much fuss and then he's standing beside me, and I've got one of the crowns on my head.

"Closer," Mick says, wagging his fingers to the right.

He comes so close he has to duck his shoulder

behind mine. My insides squeeze tight, and I'm convinced he'll feel the intense heat my cheeks and ears must be giving off. His left hand comes to rest on my waist and then I can feel his chest brushing against my back and shoulder. I try not to shiver.

"Smile!" Mick chirps.

I try, but all I can think about is if Caine is smiling. The flash goes off once and I turn my head quickly to check his expression. "Did you smile?" I ask.

"Yes, I smiled."

"Like a real smile, or like a you smile?"

That earns me the barest beginning of one. "Are you implying I don't smile like a real person?"

"I'm not implying anything. I'm saying outright you don't smile like a normal person."

He forces a giant, uncharacteristic grin and I burst into laughter.

"Oh my God, don't ever do that again."

His usual smile returns.

The flash flares to life. "If you guys aren't gonna look at me, I'm just going to take pictures of you like this," Mick admonishes.

Being reminded we're being watched makes me feel like I was doing something wrong. I press one hand to my nervous stomach and use my other hand to take the crown off.

"There. We got your picture." I ease away from Caine. "You promised."

"We don't have an official deal until the picture is in the book."

Mick lets the door to the bathroom close, plunging us into semi-darkness. The glare is gone from Caine's glasses now, so I can see into his eyes. I stare just to the point where I'm sure he knows I'm staring, then I force my eyes down. Light pressure on my fingers pulls my attention and I realize the back of his hand is brushing against mine. Tingles dance up my arm, but I can't be sure his touch isn't a quirk of our proximity. He's not doing anything more than this.

I step back and collect my camera from Mick.

He squints at me, and his eyes dart to Caine then back to me. He doesn't say anything, but the question is all over his face.

Since I have no idea what to tell him, I just say, "Thanks."

"You should keep the yearbook until you get those printed. That way I know you won't welch," Caine says.

"I would never."

"Yeah, the last time you said that, I ended up in the trunk of a clown car with a guy called Chuckles."

"Look, I tried to tell you never to trust a clown with a cookie, but would you listen?"

"I thought you said never use a clown as your bookie."

I roll my eyes. "No, you should always use a clown as your bookie. Did you not read the handbook?"

When his hand brushes against mine again, I'm certain it isn't an accident. My breath catches in my throat when he licks his lips.

"What's the name of this song?" I wonder aloud, not looking away from him.

He shakes his head slightly. "I don't know. Why?"

"We need to find out." I lean into him until I feel my skirt crimp against his legs. "Because I'm going to need a copy of it."

"You like it?"

"It doesn't matter." I smile at him. "I need it to remember."

This time, it's not the back of his hand against mine, but the softly seeking tips of his fingers curving around to graze my palm. He licks his lips again.

"M'riss!" Anna bounds into the hallway, totally oblivious to my pounding heart. "Come on, it's time for After Prom."

"What are we doing?"

She gives me a manic grin and holds out both hands, fingers beckoning for mine. I take her hand with my left, but close my fingers tight around Caine's with my right.

"You're coming, too," I tell him.

He gives me his normal, abnormal smile. "Yeah, sure."

[23]

WE ARE ON the verge of becoming criminals. Since leaving The Blue Canary, we have steadily shed members of the original group as the younger ones hit curfew. The soon-to-be-college-freshmen among us have stuck it out to the end.

So far these evening, we have:

1. Parked at the end of the runway at the airport and lay beneath the last flights in and out of the city, screaming into the deafening roar of the engines.

2. Strolled through Downtown, looking at the boats on the river and the crush of humanity outside the bars. It's summertime, and no one is wasting a moment of the nice weather.

3. Crashed a wedding reception at a posh hotel on the river. Actually, only Miguel, Myra and Sun did that, coming back with two bottles of wine and victorious grins.

4. Gone out for waffles.

5. Found a secluded part of a park to sit on the

grass and pass around our two bottles of ill-gotten wine.

There's not much wine to be had in a group of ten, but it tastes like some kind of victory, so we don't much care about the quantity. I still feel the warming effect of it on the inside of my ears and the loosey-goosey sensation in my arms. I like the way it feels.

I also really like the way it feels to be sitting hip-to-hip with Caine, our backs against the cinderblock wall of the picnic shelter where we're all hiding in shadow.

"I wish the pool was open," Myra says, gesturing to the dark entrance of the aquatic center.

"I think it is." Chris stands up and cups his hand behind one ear. "Yeah, it definitely sounds open to me."

Sun snickers. "How does a pool sound open?"

"Just like that." Chris takes off for the building and gives the turnstiles a shove. They look like giant metal scrub brushes set on end, filling the entire entryway with iron bars. They don't give an inch.

"Ooh, yeah, real open," Myra chides.

"I'm not done yet." Chris jogs around the side of the building, and then we hear the unmistakable sound of someone climbing chain link fence.

"No way." Myra's eyes go wide.

"This I gotta see." Miguel jumps to his feet and sets off at a run.

I'm the next to go, with Caine at my heels. The rest of the group isn't far behind. I make it in time to see Chris swing his leg over the top of the fence and find his footing on the inside. In five giant steps, he's on the pool deck, grinning at us.

"See? Pool's open."

Sun's the next one on the fence, jamming the toes of her platform sandals into the open weave. She's not alone for long though – everyone is going for it.

My heart is pounding while I climb. This fence is high and the metal digs hard into my bare toes, but I wasn't about to try this climb in peep-toes. Also, I can't help checking over my shoulder a million times for the police. I keep picturing one of those cop spot-lights landing on my back and the angry voice on the loudspeaker telling me to "Freeze!"

TEENS ARRESTED CLINGING TO FENCE, See Crime Watch.

It doesn't happen, though, and after a terrifying swing over the top, I'm on my way down. The ground has rarely felt so good.

"Last one in is a rotten egg!" Miguel starts shedding his suit.

Sun, Myra and Chris are the next to reach for the zippers, buttons, and clasps that keep them clothed. I'm not surprised, really. In my experience, Sun's music friends have very little shame. But Cori is the next to start, which I never saw coming. She's quick, too, getting down to her pale blue bra and underwear before anyone else has even finished unfastening.

"Losers!" she carols as she runs for the water. There's a brief splash and she calls out, "Ahh, this feels great! Hurry up, you guys!"

Miguel, Sun, Myra and Chris are next, with Anna not far behind. The only ones left on the deck are me, Deanne, Jeremy and Caine.

"Are you going in?" Deanne asks me.

"Um...."

"What the hell, we've come this far...." Jeremy starts in on his buttons.

"If you do it, I'll do it," Deanne says.

A shriek comes from the pool, but I can't see who screamed. The water has an ethereal quality to it, lit only by a series of bluish lights below the surface. It looks good. I want in.

"I'm doing it," I say. But once I've got my fingers pinched on my zipper pull, it seems a little more...daunting. I really want to check if Caine is watching me, but I will most likely die of embarrassment if he is, so I don't.

It's just like a swimsuit, it's just like a swimsuit, I

chant to myself as the top of my dress peels open to reveal the back of my bra.

Just like a strapless swimsuit.

A black satiny one.

Never mind that now. Just get in the water, that's the key. I leave my dress in a heap on the concrete deck and scamper to the water. I've never scampered before, but I am positive that's what I'm doing now. I'm a woodland creature. Not a graceful one, like a deer. More of a raccoon.

Who cares?

I pinch my nose and jump into the six-foot section – hair and make-up be damned. While I'm still underwater, I hear the *shooshing* of the others plunging in to the water after me. I come up, drifting into a back float and staring up at the stars. The air feels cool compared to the August-heated water, so I give up some buoyancy to leave only my face above the surface. Overhead, the late summer stars look close enough to touch and impossibly far at the same time.

Night swimming is one of life's great pleasures.

All around I hear the sounds of lapping water and quiet laughter. I shift to treading water, looking around at the other dark heads bobbing around me. It's hard to recognize everyone now that they're all wet and scattered in the dim glow of the underwater lights. I squint at the person closest to me and do a double-take.

"You're not wearing your glasses." I paddle toward Caine, who turns toward me with the vacant eyes of the nearsighted.

"I lost a pair of glasses in the bottom of a pool once."

"Loch Ness Monster?" I ask.

"Mermaids."

"Notorious thieves." When I get closer, I tread water, feeling the current of his churning arms and legs near mine.

"Ah, I can see you again," he says, blinking at me.

I push a lank section of hair out of my face. "Maybe I should have stayed back there. I'm a mess."

"We all are." He does the one-handed hair shoving move and winces when his fingers catch in his wet curls. Suddenly his face brightens and he stops moving constantly in the water. "I can stand here."

I slow my kicking and stretch for the bottom, but my head slips under before I can reach. "I can't."

He stretches out a submerged hand and catches my forearm. It's not quite enough to keep me up so I grab him by the elbow with my other hand. My stomach flutters.

"So, has it been as insufferable as you imagined?" I ask.

"Tonight?" He shakes his head. "It's actually been...fun."

I smile. "Good."

I've stopped kicking my legs and now they bump into his as I drift in the water. For once, I don't jump away. I flex one foot and run my toes down his shin.

"I have to thank you," I tell him.

"For what?"

"There will never be a picture or a ticket stub or a wristband or a birthday card for this moment. Right here, right now. But I know I'll never forget it." I smile at him. "You helped me learn that."

He looks down and his hand lands on my hip. Even dressed in hundreds of gallons of water, it feels intense and intimate in my underwear. I bite my lip.

"You know you're a lot more Spiderman than Peter Parker," he says.

"What?" I laugh quietly, like I'm in the library.

"I don't know how I missed it. But you make things happen."

"Not hardly." My cheeks are hot again.

"Look at where we are."

"This is Chris's fault," I say.

"No. You're the reason we're here. You."

I survey the pool again, but just for a moment. I

don't want to pull my eyes away from him for too long. "I have good friends." I smile at him. "And I'm really, really glad you're one of them." Then a moment of panic strikes me and the smile slips. "We are friends, aren't we?"

"Yeah, sure." Barely more than a breath.

I slide my hands up to hold his shoulders. Even in the water he's so much warmer than me.

"Mariska...." He sighs and tries again. "I couldn't have thrown the yearbook away."

My toes slide along his shins again. We're only touching at a handful of contact points, but I swear the water swirling between us warmer than the rest of the pool.

"You actually made me want to keep that pointless hunk of paper."

I laugh. "Sorry."

"Don't be." A brief, rusty bark of laughter escapes him and I feel a rush of pleasure. His rare laughter has been causing that lately. "I'm gonna have to get used to caring about something I own again."

"Maybe you should just get a really big fireproof box." I lift my hands from his shoulders to imagine a small safe in the air between us.

"I don't know...I think I might like the risk factor."

I raise my eyebrows. "You adrenaline junkie. Next thing you'll be bungie jumping *with* your glasses on."

The ghost-smile makes an appearance. "I have something else in mind."

"Blindfolded trust walk on the edge of a cliff?" I widen my eyes and press my toes hard into his legs.

"No." He closes the distance between us until his nose bumps my cheek and my bare stomach is pressed to his.

Stupidly, I say, "Oh!" just before he kisses me.

The melting feeling floods through me again. He tastes like wine and chlorine, and nothing has ever tasted so good. His arms wind around my back and there's so much warmth everywhere he touches me. Water droplets run down from his hair, tracing the contour of his cheek and coming to rest in the corner of my lips. The sound of our friends' laughter and splashing is distant and receding all the time, because this is the center of my universe right now.

A smattering of applause finally brings us back to reality, and we break apart, laughing. Well, I'm laughing. Caine's smiling – a little more than usual, I notice.

"Mariska and Ca-aine, sittin' in a tree…" Sun chants.

I laugh again, and slide my hands up the back of his neck. He closes his eyes and presses into my touch for a moment before pulling me into another kiss. And I think that's a great idea.

EPILOGUE

When my Spanish class lets out, I'm the first one out the door. I have a train to catch, and exactly six minutes to get to the station or I'll have to wait for the next one. It's chillier now than when I went into class and the sun is already setting. I zip my jacket and stuff my hands in my pockets as I weave through the crowd of students on the sidewalk.

The 'L' station is surprisingly empty for a Friday, and I wonder if I missed my train. But the rumbling sound in the distance says otherwise. Yay! I go as close as I dare to the tracks, as if those nanoseconds will make my journey faster, but I can't help it. The wind created by the train blows my hair into my face, which makes me think I should have brought a hat, but then I'm on the train and I don't care anymore.

Twenty-one minutes. That's all I have to survive. Twenty-one long, slow minutes filled with other people's coughing, half-heard cell phone conversations, and the *cha-*

chunk cha-chunk of the tracks below.

I drum my fingers on my knees and do a mental inventory of my backpack. I wish I didn't have my Spanish books with me. I hate the thought of them banging into my camera. I've already started amassing a pretty spectacular collection of pictures of the inside of my lens cap in the last two-and-a-half months.

A quick phone check reveals a new message from Sun. It's a picture of her face smashed in next to another girl. She's a bleached blond with a pierced nose and a wide smile. The caption: *So cute, right?* I snap a picture of my hand giving a thumbs-up and send it as reply.

I've got e-mail from Anna, Liv and Maddy, and one from my mom, as well as a fine selection of junk mail and forwards from Ray. Ray should have a spam filter on his outbox.

The train slows for my stop, so I don't bother reading anything right now. I get to my feet at just the wrong moment and lose my balance, slamming my shoulder into one of the upright railings as the train lurches to a halt. I'm the first one off, though, so I chalk this one into the win column. Even if it did pull back the mask on my I-am-a-smooth-Chicago-native facade.

Only blocks to go now, so I send a warning text as I eat up the sidewalk.

At last I'm in the lobby of McCabe hall and Caine is waiting for me. I give him my biggest smile and get one that even shows some teeth in return. He's been smiling a lot bigger lately.

I think it might have something to do with me.

He catches my hand and gives me a quick yank until I'm close enough for a kiss on the cheek.

"Come on, let's check you in."

We go to the front desk and I show ID so they'll let me in the building, then we take the stairs to the third floor. The people who live on the higher floors tend to get resentful of anyone on the bottom three floors using the elevator.

The door to Caine's suite is standing open and two of his roommates are planted in front of a Playstation 3.

"Hey, Mariska," one of the guys, Cameron, says.

"Hey guys!" I wave, but they can't look away from the first-person shooter game.

Caine heads down the hall to his room – a single, the lucky bastard. He only got it because he told the other guys he's a neat freak. He's not really. He just doesn't have enough stuff to make a mess with. His dorm room is a smaller version of his bedroom in his parents' house, except he has a bigger computer monitor now. Also, the infamous yearbook sits on the top shelf above his desk. It's so swamped with additions now, the cover is at a sixty-degree angle to the back.

Seeing it reminds me. "I have something for you," I say, dropping my backpack and coat on the end of his bed.

"Just a second." He slides an arm around my waist and kisses me on the mouth now that we're alone.

My eyes drift shut and I savor the sinking, melting feeling he always gives me. My favorite part about Caine is that I always feel like he's kissing me, not just my lips. Like it's not just kissing for kissing's sake.

He pulls back. "Okay, what'd you bring?"

"Greedy, greedy." I smile at him while I dig through the clothes I have packed in my bag until I find the burned CD tucked into the fold of a sweater. "Put it in. Track three."

He feeds the disc into his computer and clicks ahead twice when the music starts.

The track begins with the static of a worn record, then a muted brass section defines the rhythm before the rest of the orchestra sweeps in with a melody that sounds the way a violin looks, if that makes any sense. Finally a smoky, sultry woman's voice joins, singing the simple lyrics.

> *Gonna take a sentimental journey*
> *Gonna set my heart at ease.*

*Gonna make a sentimental journey
To renew old memories.*

Caine looks confused, but I can tell he's thinking hard.

"It's the song. From the Blue Canary."

Slowly, his face relaxes and he nods. "Yeah, sure. I hear it now."

"I found it."

"Of course you did." He rubs his thumb over my wrist. "Sentimental Mariska."

"It's going in the book." I nod at the shelving unit, where the yearbook is about to open its maw just a little larger.

He gives me the new, slightly larger version of the ghost-smile. "You can't glue music to paper."

"I can sure glue a CD case to paper, though."

He sighs, but it's a thoughtful sigh rather than his impatient one. I'm getting more fluent by the day in his quiet language. "All right. It's going in."

"Good." I nod firmly, then lean in until my head is on his shoulder and swing my arms around his back. "Missed you."

"Missed you, too." He leans his head on mine and sighs again. A contented one this time. "You're staying, right?"

"I have to. The witness protection program is relocating me here, didn't I mention that?"

"I was wondering about that FBI guy following me this week."

"I would have warned you, but...unsecured lines. You know."

"Right." He rubs my back with one hand.

The music is still playing, old-fashioned and smooth. It takes me a moment to realize he's swaying just a little. I lift my head to squint at him.

"Are you dancing?"

"Absolutely not."

"Okay, just checking." I add my own sway to his, and close my eyes, soaking in the moment.

And just like that, this song has yet another little memory locked up in its notes from this point forward.

You never can tell what's going to matter in the future, and slowly but surely I'm learning to love that. The only thing I can do is keep my eyes open and pay attention.

AUTHOR'S NOTE

ALTHOUGH MANY OF the locations in Throwing My Life Away are or were real, some of them have been relegated to memory long before the timeline of this story. Others are an amalgamation of existing places, or have been relocated from their actual homes in Milwaukee to suit my whims.

Many thanks to my friends, from the past and present, who helped shape this story and my life. You are all unicorns.

Extra special sparkling rainbow unicorn horns to:

Liz Lincoln, for copyediting and general awesomeness.

Sarah from Okay Creations for this gorgeous cover.

My Hideaway Banditas for support, encouragement and patience.

Laura Bradford for working her butt off for me all the time, and especially on this project.

My family. The whole lot of you.

ABOUT THE AUTHOR

LIZ CZUKAS is the author of *Ask Again Later* and *Top Ten Clues You're Clueless*, as well as several romantic comedies under the penname Ellie Cahill. She lives outside Milwaukee, WI with her family and the happiest golden retriever in the world.

http://www.lizczukas.com
Twitter: @lizczukas

ALWAYS BE FIRST. JOIN THE NEWSLETTER.

BE THE FIRST to know when Liz has a deal or a new book you don't want to miss: You can sign up at lizczukas.com.

IF YOU LIKED what you just read, please considering taking a few minutes to share a review at your favorite retailer. You can't imagine what a difference it makes to authors.

Thanks for reading. I think you're swell.

www.ingramcontent.com/pod-product-compliance
Lightning Source LLC
Chambersburg PA
CBHW030606170726
48283CB00002B/483